BARB·WIRE

writer **John Arcudi**

pencillers **Dan Lawlis & Mike Manley**

inkers **Ian Akin & Ande Parks**

colorist **Pamela Rambo**

letterer **Pat Brosseau**

series editor **Michael Eury**

series assistant editor **Marilee Hord**

collection editor **Lynn Adair**

collection designer **Harald Graham**

collection manager **Brian Gogolin**

Barb Wire™ created by **Chris Warner**

TITAN BOOKS

publisher	**Mike Richardson**
executive vice president	**Neil Hankerson**
vice president of publishing	**David Scroggy**
vice president of sales & marketing	**Lou Bank**
vice president of finance	**Andy Karabatsos**
general counsel	**Mark Anderson**
creative director	**Randy Stradley**
director of production & design	**Cindy Marks**
art director	**Mark Cox**
computer graphics director	**Sean Tierney**
director of accounting	**Chris Creviston**
marketing director	**Michael Martens**
sales & licensing director	**Tod Borleske**
director of operations	**Mark Ellington**
director of m.i.s.	**Dale LaFountain**

This book collects issues two, three, five, and six of the Dark Horse comic-book series *Barb Wire*™.

Published by Titan Books Ltd,
42-44 Dolben Street,
London SE1 0UP by arrangement
with Dark Horse Comics.

First UK edition
March 1996
ISBN: 1 85286 710 8

10 9 8 7 6 5 4 3 2 1
Printed in Canada

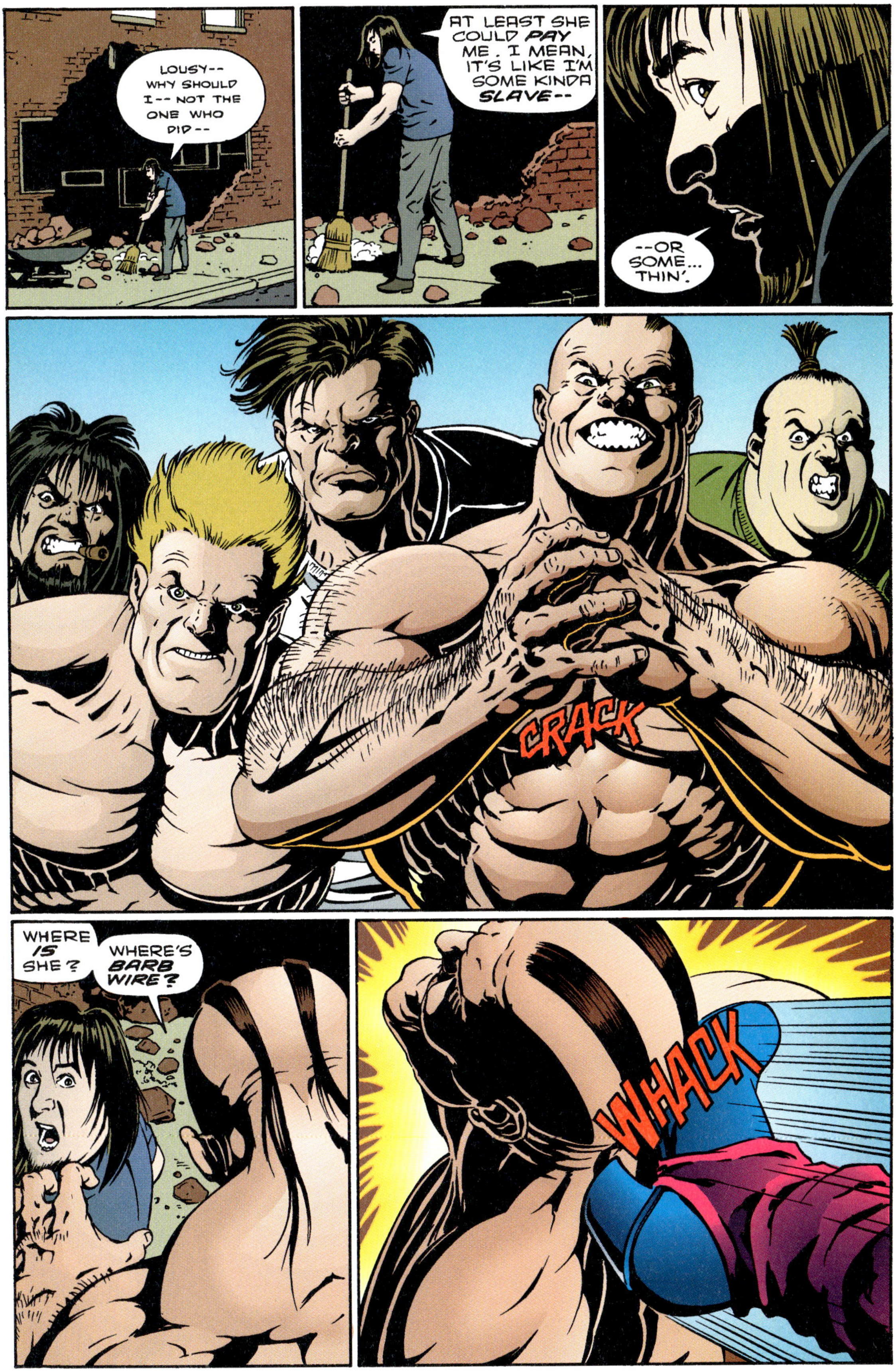

LOUSY-- WHY SHOULD I-- NOT THE ONE WHO DID--

AT LEAST SHE COULD *PAY* ME. I MEAN, IT'S LIKE I'M SOME KINDA *SLAVE*--

--OR SOME... THIN'.

WHERE *IS* SHE? WHERE'S *BARB WIRE*?

CRACK

WHACK

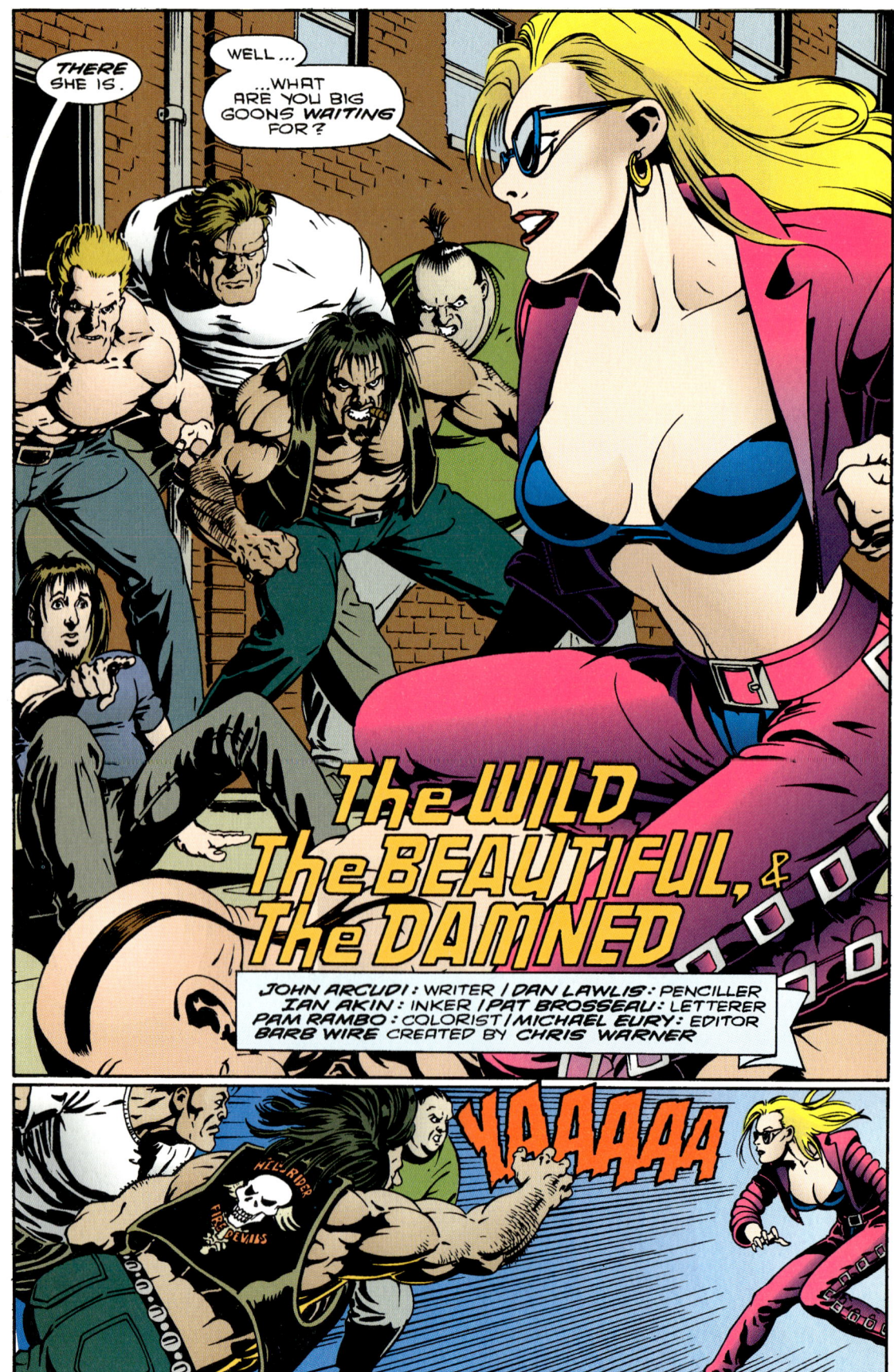

The WILD The BEAUTIFUL, & The DAMNED

JOHN ARCUDI: WRITER / DAN LAWLIS: PENCILLER
IAN AKIN: INKER / PAT BROSSEAU: LETTERER
PAM RAMBO: COLORIST / MICHAEL EURY: EDITOR
BARB WIRE CREATED BY CHRIS WARNER

SPEED IT *UP*, GUYS. I HAVEN'T GOT ALL DAY.

THWAK

OH, NOT *BAD*...

HUOUHH!

...BUT NOT VERY *GOOD*, EITHER.

LADY, I DON'T LIKE YOUR *JOKES* MUCH.

I NEVER SAID I WAS MUCH OF A *COMEDIENNE*, "BLUTO" --

FIFTEEN SECONDS.

THIRTY.

FORTY-FIVE SECONDS. FOR *BARB WIRE*, THIS IS A VERY LONG FIGHT.

YEAH, THAT'S IT... KEEP THE COCKY LITTLE TWIST *BUSY*.

THEN I'LL SEE IF HER *SKULL* IS AS TOUGH AS HER *MOUTH*.

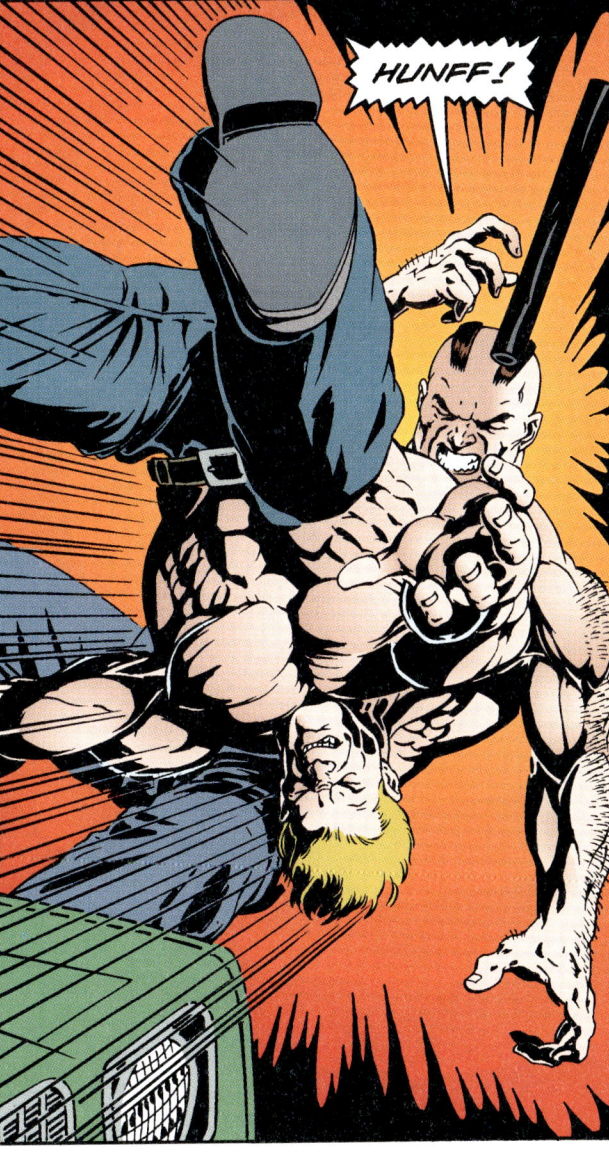

HUNFF!

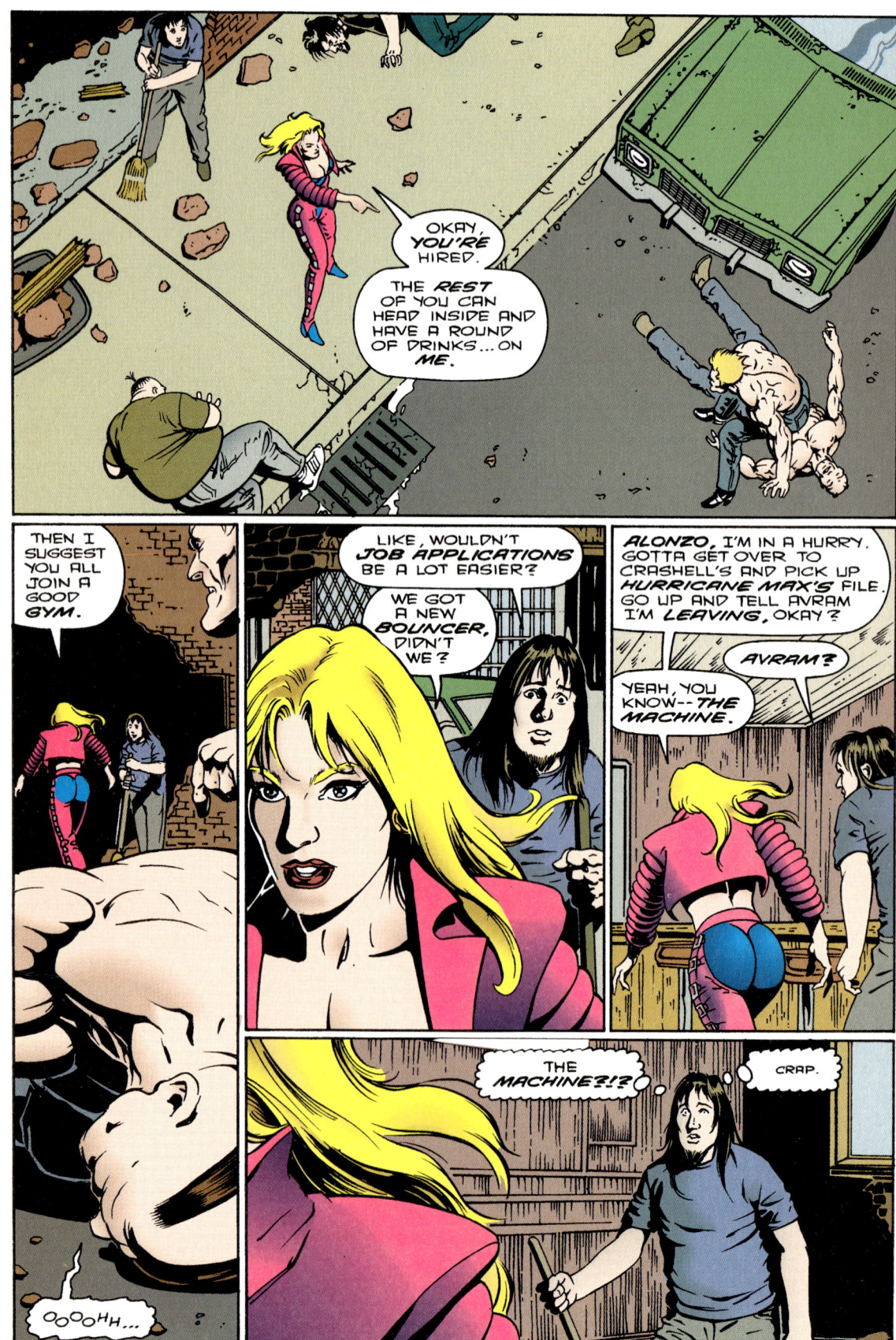

ACROSS TOWN, AT WOOD-HULL GENERAL, *IGNITION* IS TAKING ONE MORE DAY TO DIE.

EXCUSE ME?

WHAT DO YOU WANT?

IT'S TIME FOR MR. MACK'S *SPONGE BATH.*

OH, *YOU'D* LIKE THAT, WOULDN'T YOU?

GETTIN' ALL WET AND NAKED WITH A *PRETTY* NURSE.

MISS, ARE-- ARE YOU *FEELING* ALL RIGHT?

GET *OUTTA* HERE, YOU STARCHED LINEN *SLUT!*

AND IF I CATCH ANY OF YOU TRAMPS MESSIN' WITH MY MAN--

--I'LL *KILL* YOU!!!

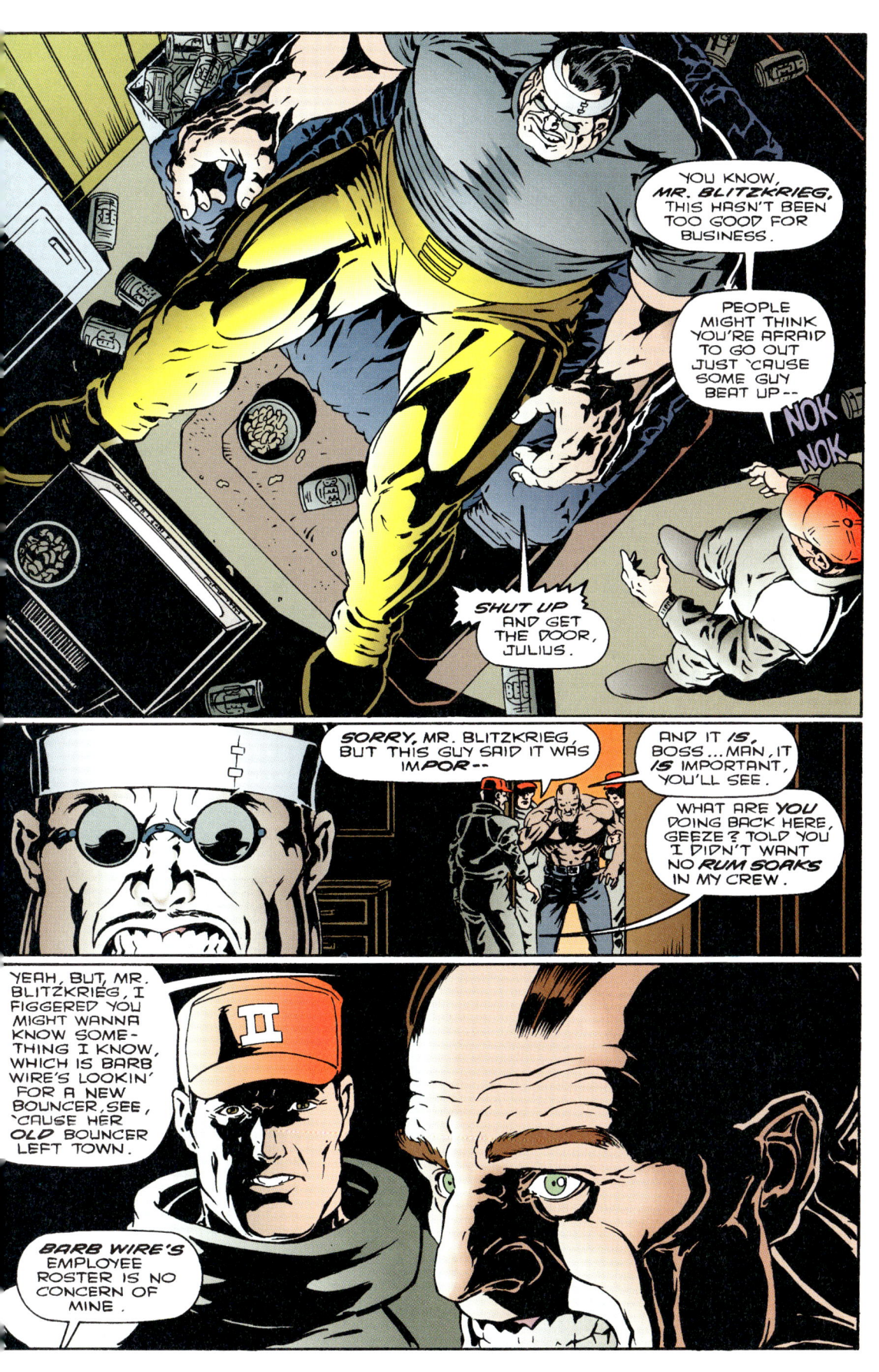

FRANK FLETCHER.

SUPER.

FAN BELT *AND* RADIATOR GONE. 'COURSE, DRIVING AIMLESSLY THROUGH THE NEVADA DESERT FOR HOURS IS BOUND TO DO THAT TO *ANY* CAR.

WONDER WHAT THEY'RE DOING IN *STEEL HARBOR* RIGHT NOW? MAYBE THEY'RE WONDERING WHAT *I'M* DOING.

YEAH, RIGHT... BARB'S PROBABLY ALREADY *REPLACED* ME AT THE BAR.

PROBABLY THROWING A BIG *PARTY*, CELEBRATING MY LEAVING.

OH, NOW DON'T START WITH *THAT* CRAP AGAIN.

I MUSTA BEEN *CRAZY*, LETTING YOU TALK ME INTO COMING OUT HERE. *YOU* DON'T EVEN KNOW WHERE WE'RE GOING, *DO* YOU?

UH-HUH. "OVER THE NEXT HILL." *SURE.*

YOU SAID THAT ABOUT AN *HOUR* AGO, TOO.

WHAT?

WELL, YOU DIDN'T EXPECT ME TO *WALK*, DID YOU?

SUBJECT: MAXWELL HIDALGO, ALIAS: *HURRICANE MAX.*

STATUS: *PARANORMAL.* CAN GENERATE WINDS IN EXCESS OF 110 MPH WITHOUT APPARENT AID OF ANY APPARATUS.

UPWARD LIMITS OF PARANORMAL ABILITIES: *UNKNOWN.*

WANTED IN CONNECTION WITH NUMEROUS ROBBERIES, ARSONS, ASSAULTS. SUBJECT IS RARELY ARMED, BUT SHOULD BE CONSIDERED *EXTREMELY DANGEROUS.*

--BUT IS *HUMAN* IN ALL OTHER RESPECTS AND CAN BE INCAPACITATED BY CONVENTIONAL MEANS AT CLOSE RANGE.

REMARKS: SUBJECT'S ABILITIES CAN *REPEL* MOST FORMS OF ATTACK--

THE *ELEMENT OF SURPRISE* SHOULD BE USEFUL IN PREVENTING SUBJECT'S EMPLOYMENT OF SAID ABILITIES.

CHUK

SURPRISE.

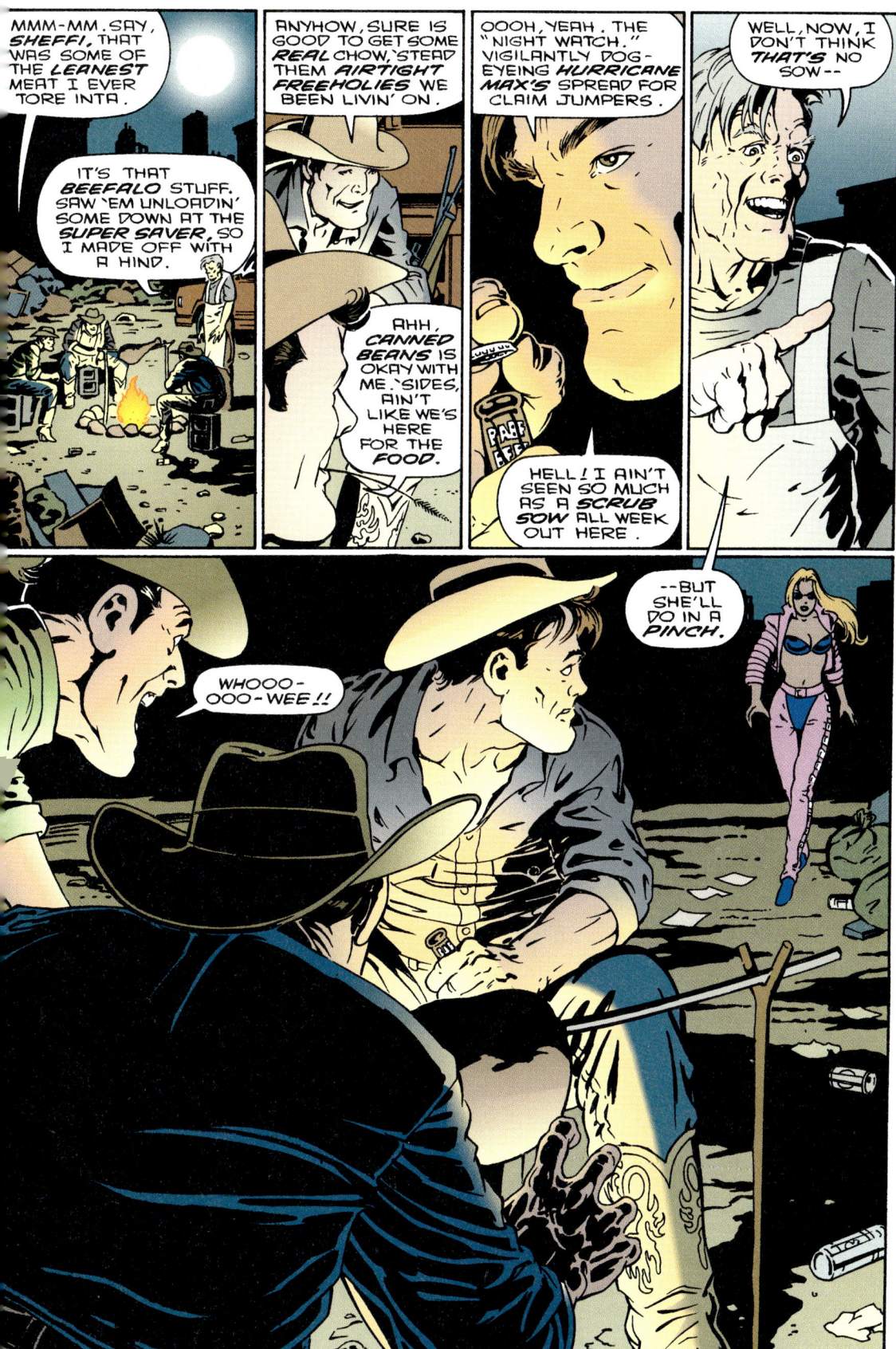

FREEZE!

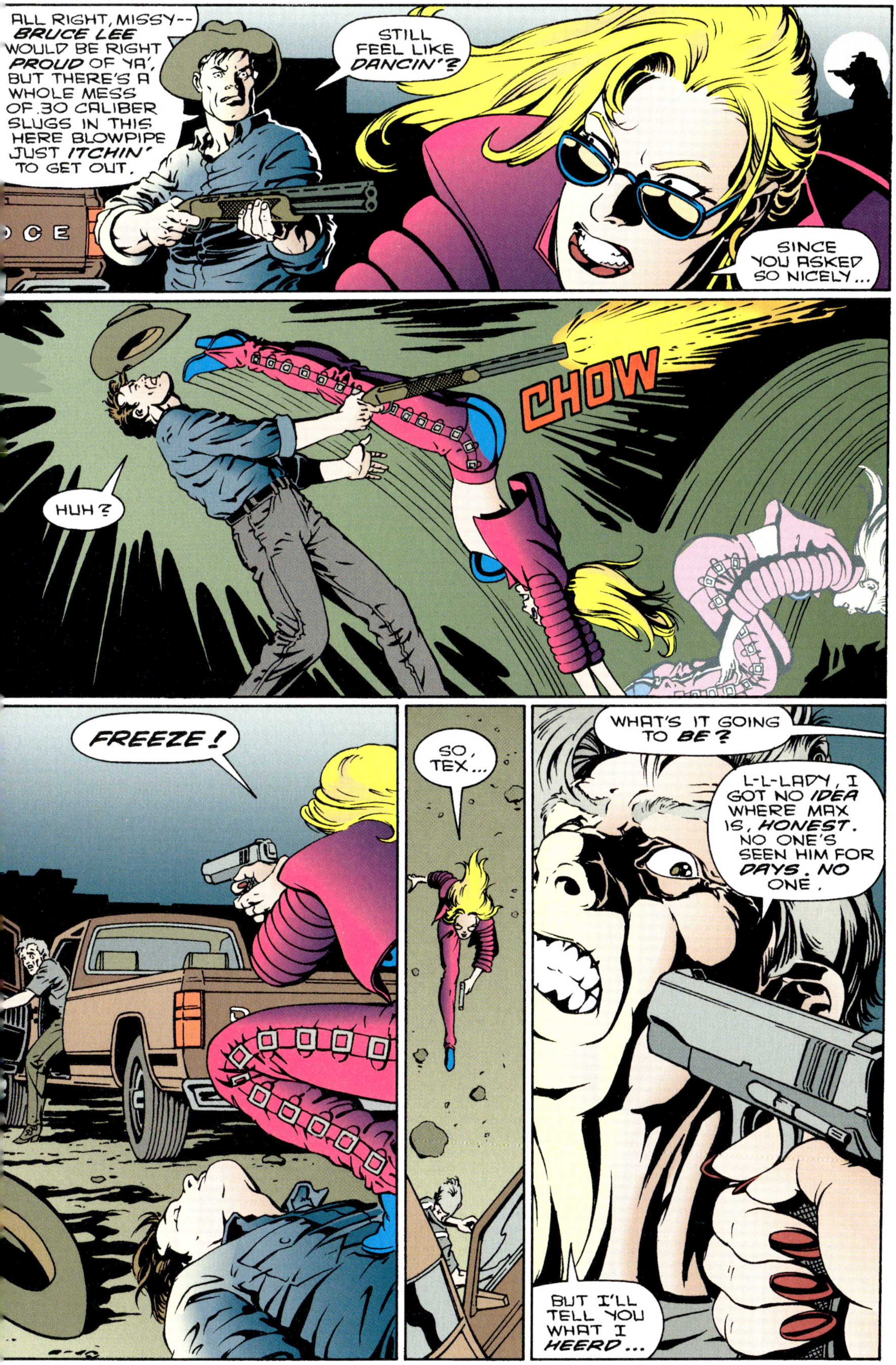

SO, TEX...

WHAT'S IT GOING TO *BE*?

L-L-LADY, I GOT NO *IDEA* WHERE MAX IS, *HONEST*. NO ONE'S SEEN HIM FOR *DAYS*. NO ONE.

BUT I'LL TELL YOU WHAT I *HEERD*...

SOON...

YEAH, I THINK I HAVE A *LEAD*. I'M HEADING OVER TO *WOODHULL HOSPITAL*.

YOU GOT ANYTHING?

NOTHING...

BARBARA, PLEASE DON'T SEND ALONZO UP TO MY ROOM ANYMORE.

HE'S AFRAID OF ME.

ALL RIGHT, SORRY ABOUT THAT. I'LL HAVE A *TALK* WITH HIM.

PLEASE-- DON'T.

JUST... JUST DON'T SEND HIM UP ANYMORE.

SURE THING, AVRAM. WHATEVER YOU *SAY*.

OKAY, I'M TAKING OFF. JUST STAY HOOKED INTO THE *PHONE LINES*. LET ME KNOW IF YOU *HEAR* ANYTHING.

OF COURSE, BARBARA.

THAT'S WHAT I DO--

--ISN'T IT?

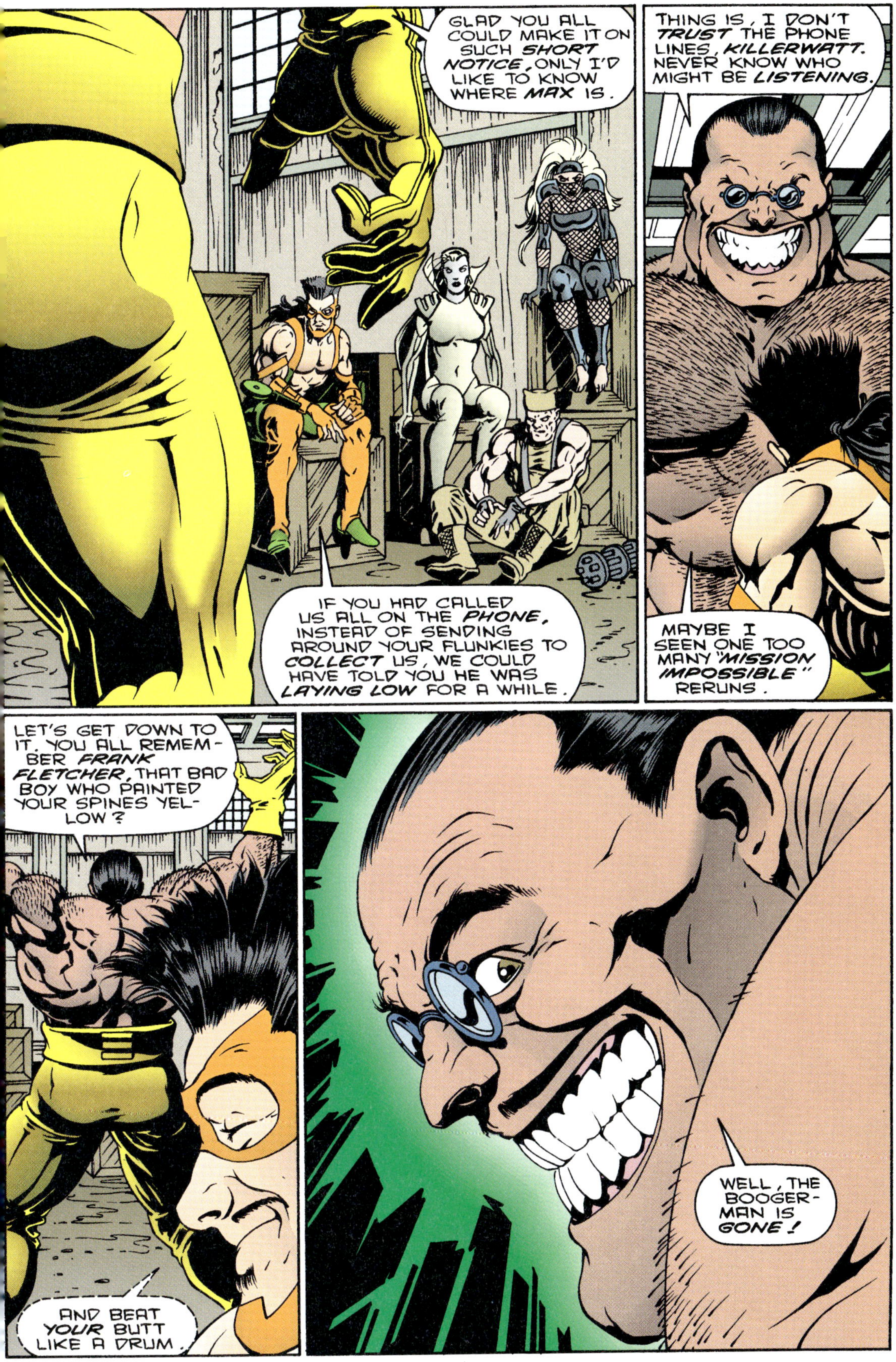

GLAD YOU ALL COULD MAKE IT ON SUCH *SHORT NOTICE*, ONLY I'D LIKE TO KNOW WHERE *MAX* IS.

THING IS, I DON'T *TRUST* THE PHONE LINES, *KILLERWATT*. NEVER KNOW WHO MIGHT BE *LISTENING*.

IF YOU HAD CALLED US ALL ON THE *PHONE*, INSTEAD OF SENDING AROUND YOUR FLUNKIES TO *COLLECT* US, WE COULD HAVE TOLD YOU HE WAS *LAYING LOW* FOR A WHILE.

MAYBE I SEEN ONE TOO MANY *"MISSION IMPOSSIBLE"* RERUNS.

LET'S GET DOWN TO IT. YOU ALL REMEMBER *FRANK FLETCHER*, THAT BAD BOY WHO PAINTED YOUR SPINES YELLOW?

AND BEAT *YOUR* BUTT LIKE A DRUM.

WELL, THE BOOGERMAN IS *GONE!*

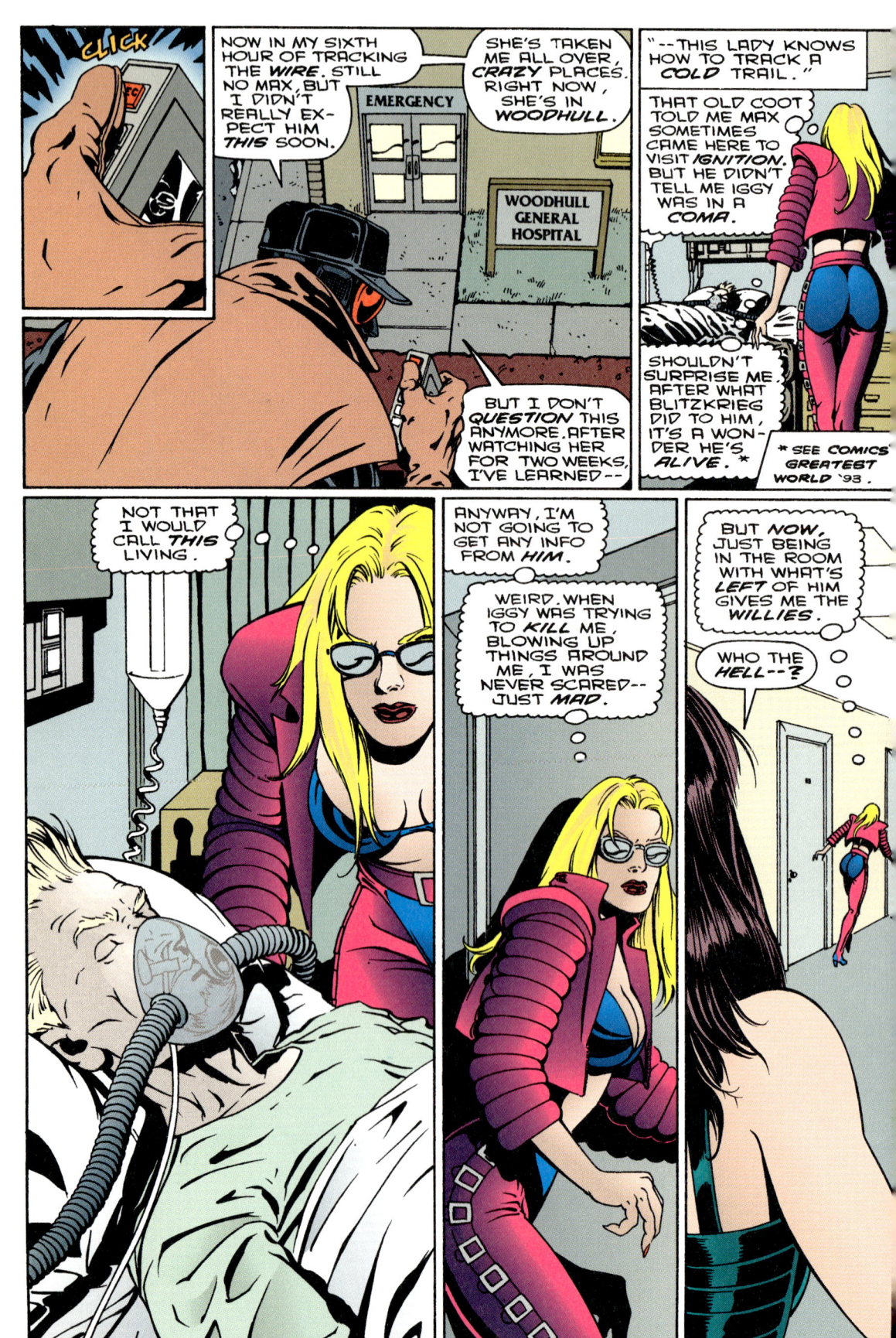

CLICK

NOW IN MY SIXTH HOUR OF TRACKING THE *WIRE*. STILL NO MAX, BUT I DIDN'T REALLY EXPECT HIM *THIS* SOON.

SHE'S TAKEN ME ALL OVER, *CRAZY* PLACES. RIGHT NOW, SHE'S IN *WOODHULL*.

EMERGENCY

WOODHULL GENERAL HOSPITAL

BUT I DON'T *QUESTION* THIS ANYMORE. AFTER WATCHING HER FOR TWO WEEKS, I'VE LEARNED--

"--THIS LADY KNOWS HOW TO TRACK A *COLD* TRAIL."

THAT OLD COOT TOLD ME MAX SOMETIMES CAME HERE TO VISIT *IGNITION*. BUT HE DIDN'T TELL ME IGGY WAS IN A *COMA*.

SHOULDN'T SURPRISE ME, AFTER WHAT BLITZKRIEG DID TO HIM, IT'S A WONDER HE'S *ALIVE*. *

* SEE *COMICS GREATEST WORLD* '93.

NOT THAT I WOULD CALL *THIS* LIVING.

ANYWAY, I'M NOT GOING TO GET ANY INFO FROM *HIM*.

WEIRD. WHEN IGGY WAS TRYING TO *KILL* ME, BLOWING UP THINGS AROUND ME, I WAS NEVER SCARED-- JUST *MAD*.

BUT *NOW*, JUST BEING IN THE ROOM WITH WHAT'S *LEFT* OF HIM GIVES ME THE *WILLIES*.

WHO THE *HELL*--?

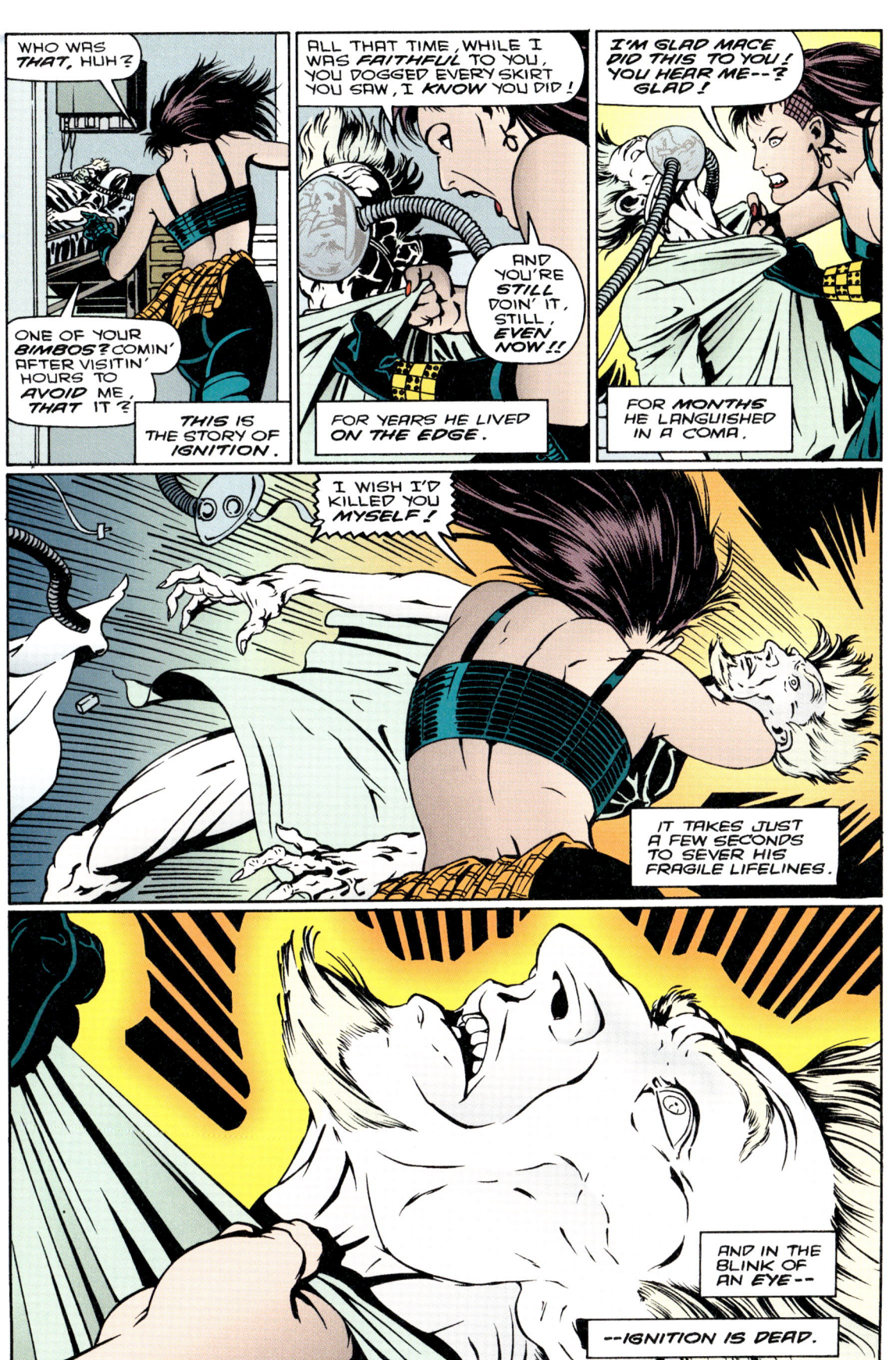

CYCLE OF FIRE

JOHN ARCUDI WRITER

DAN LAWLIS PENCILLER

IAN AKIN INKER

PAT BROSSEAU LETTERER

PAM RAMBO COLORIST

M. HORD ASST. EDITOR

MICHAEL EURY EDITOR

BARB WIRE CREATED BY CHRIS WARNER

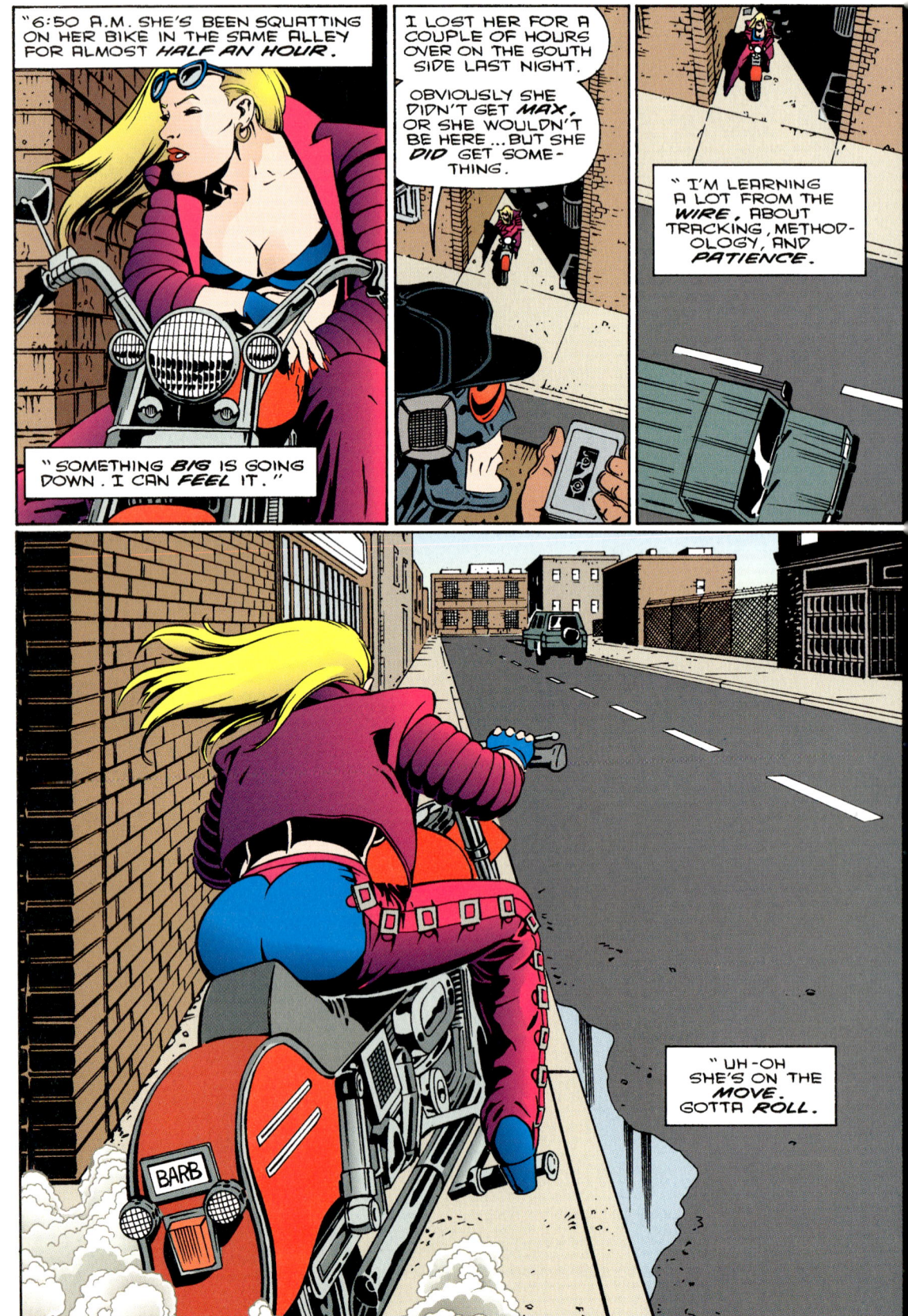

THERE'S MORE'N ONE WAY TO ROPE A DOGIE.
A RECORDING?!? A FRIGGING RECORDING?!
WHAT THE HELL'S GOING ON HERE?!
CLICK
THAT, "G.I. JOE," WAS NOT A RECORDING.

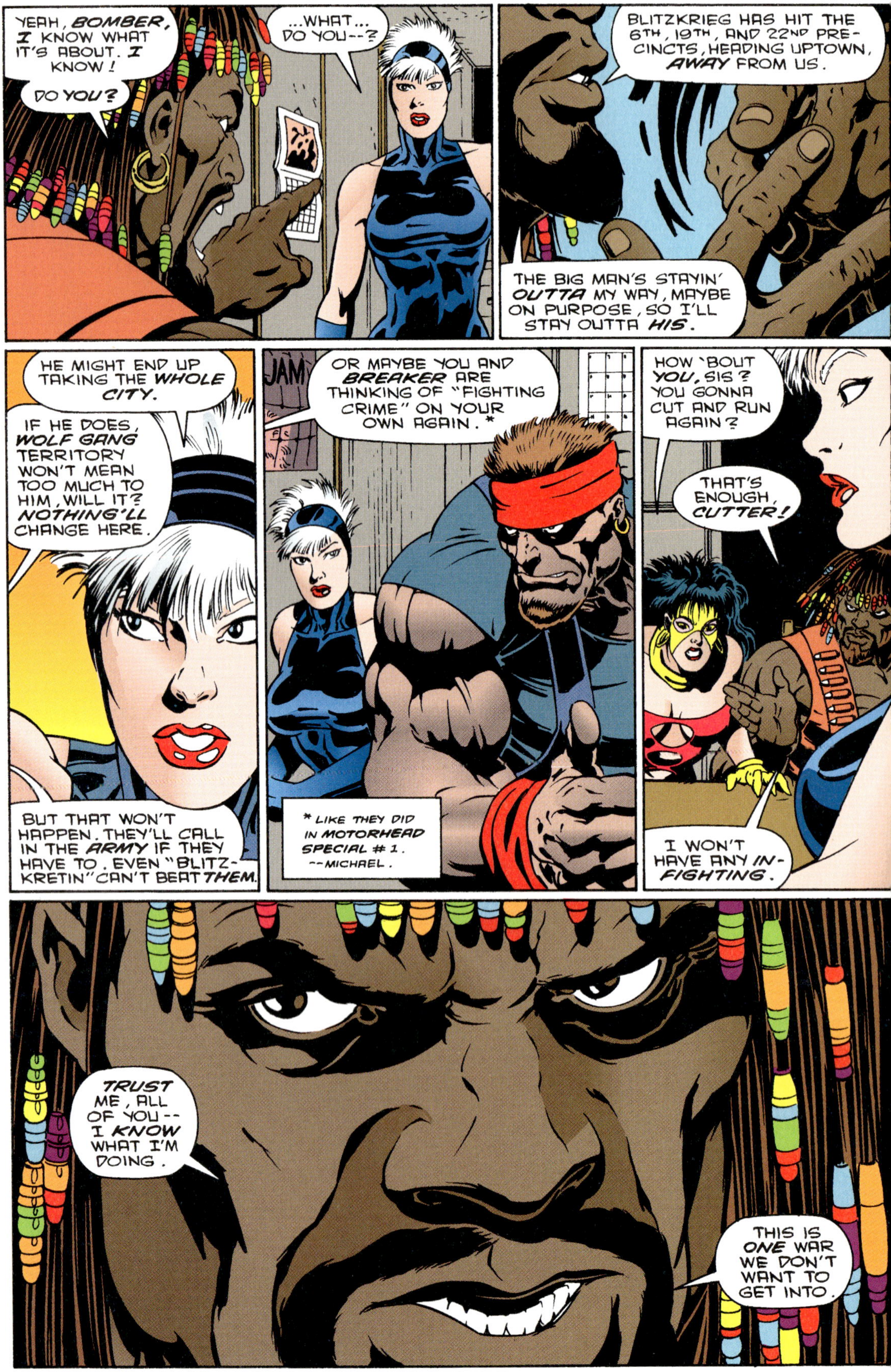

YEAH, *BOMBER,* *I* KNOW WHAT IT'S ABOUT. *I* KNOW!

DO YOU?

...WHAT... DO YOU--?

BLITZKRIEG HAS HIT THE 6TH, 19TH, AND 22ND PRE-CINCTS, HEADING UPTOWN, *AWAY* FROM US.

THE BIG MAN'S STAYIN' *OUTTA* MY WAY, MAYBE ON PURPOSE, SO I'LL STAY OUTTA *HIS.*

HE MIGHT END UP TAKING THE *WHOLE* CITY.

IF HE DOES, *WOLF GANG* TERRITORY WON'T MEAN TOO MUCH TO HIM, WILL IT? *NOTHING'LL* CHANGE HERE.

BUT THAT WON'T HAPPEN. THEY'LL CALL IN THE *ARMY* IF THEY HAVE TO. EVEN "BLITZ-KRETIN" CAN'T BEAT *THEM.*

OR MAYBE YOU AND *BREAKER* ARE THINKING OF "FIGHTING CRIME" ON YOUR OWN AGAIN. *

* LIKE THEY DID IN *MOTORHEAD SPECIAL* #1. --MICHAEL.

HOW 'BOUT *YOU,* SIS? YOU GONNA CUT AND RUN AGAIN?

THAT'S ENOUGH, *CUTTER!*

I WON'T HAVE ANY IN-FIGHTING.

TRUST ME, ALL OF YOU-- I *KNOW* WHAT I'M DOING.

THIS IS *ONE WAR* WE DON'T WANT TO GET INTO.

7:47 A.M.

STUPID, STUPID, STUPID! HOW COULD I THINK A HUNTER LIKE YOU WOULDN'T SPOT ME?

JUST DROP THE GUN.

YOU GOT A NAME?

A FEW. THE ONLY ONE YOU NEED TO KNOW IS DEATH-CARD.

UH-HUH, THAT'S THE SHELL, ALL RIGHT -- AND ONLY ONE?

ONE'S ALL I NEED.

I'M REAL FREAKING IMPRESSED.

LISTEN-- I DON'T LIKE FOLKS FOLLOWING ME AROUND AND KILLING OFF MY JUMPERS AS I SPOT 'EM. I FIND IT UNSETTLING.

I GOT A JOB TO DO, AND IT JUST SO HAPPENS THAT YOUR TRACKING SKILLS CAN MAKE THAT JOB EASIER. I'D BE A FOOL IF I DIDN'T EXPLOIT THAT.

"JOB"? YOU MEAN YOU'RE GETTING PAID FOR THIS?

THAT'S NOT WHAT I MEAN AT ALL. LOOK, MAYBE WE CAN WORK SOMETHING OUT.

I KNOW YOU CAN COLLECT A BOUNTY ON HURRICANE MAX, DEAD OR ALIVE.

I JUST WANT HIM DEAD. YOU CAN HAVE HIM AFTER THAT.

SO, WHERE IS HE?

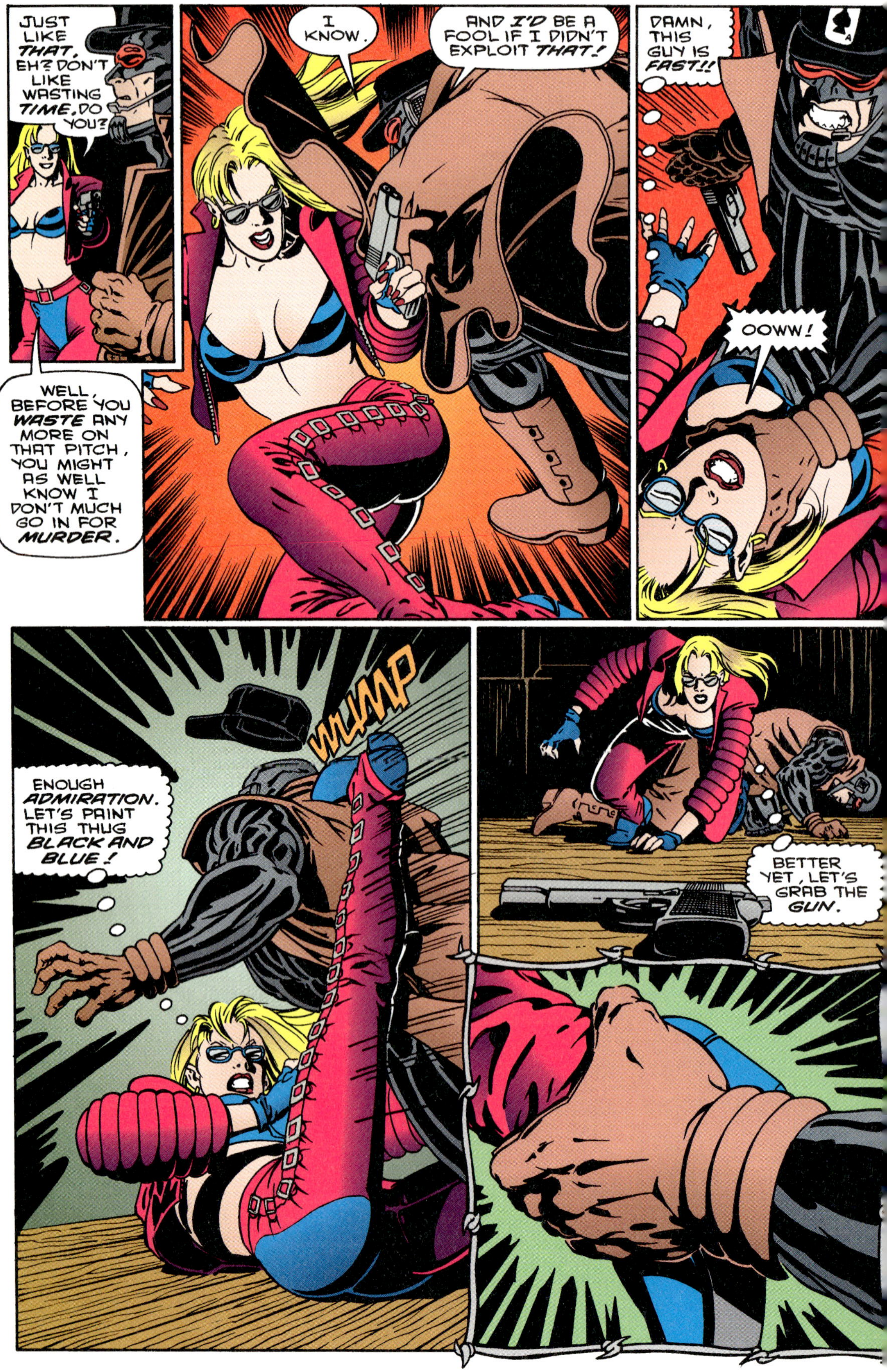
JUST LIKE THAT, EH? DON'T LIKE WASTING TIME, DO YOU?
WELL, BEFORE YOU WASTE ANY MORE ON THAT PITCH, YOU MIGHT AS WELL KNOW I DON'T MUCH GO IN FOR MURDER.
I KNOW.
AND I'D BE A FOOL IF I DIDN'T EXPLOIT THAT!
DAMN, THIS GUY IS FAST!!
OOWW!
ENOUGH ADMIRATION. LET'S PAINT THIS THUG BLACK AND BLUE!
WUMP
BETTER YET, LET'S GRAB THE GUN.

NO, JUST *PEOPLE.*

I THOUGHT YOU ONLY NEEDED *ONE* BULLET.

FOR THE RATS AND THE ROACHES. FOR THE *WOLVES,* I ALWAYS STRAP ON A LITTLE *EXTRA.*

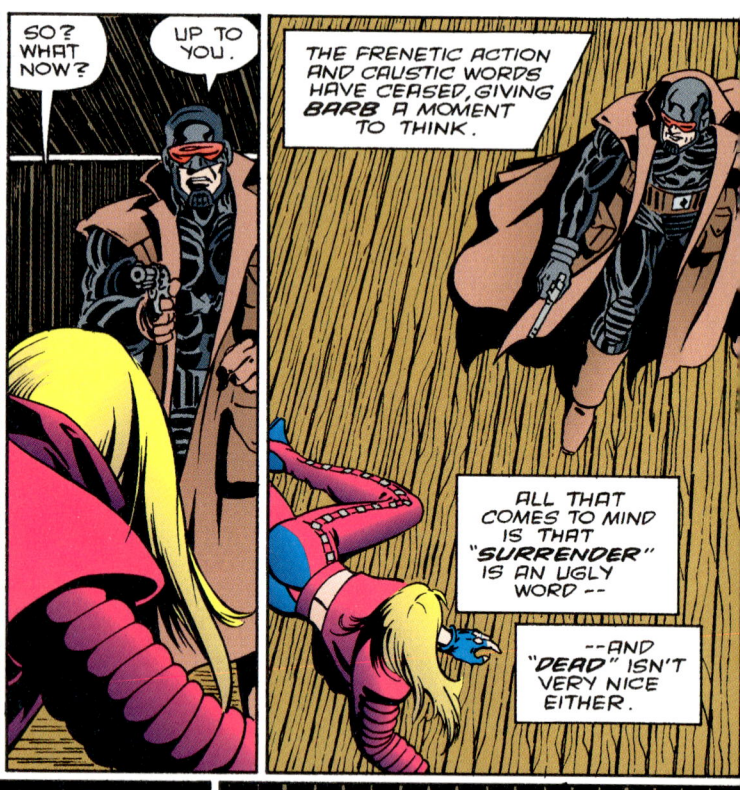

SO? WHAT NOW?

UP TO YOU.

THE FRENETIC ACTION AND CAUSTIC WORDS HAVE CEASED, GIVING *BARB* A MOMENT TO THINK.

ALL THAT COMES TO MIND IS THAT *"SURRENDER"* IS AN UGLY WORD --

--AND *"DEAD"* ISN'T VERY NICE EITHER.

TIME CREEPS ALONG ALMOST IMPERCEPTIBLY ON UNSTEADY FINGERS...

...PULLING TOWARDS SOMETHING UNSURE, UNNAMED --

-- AND, AS YET, *UNREACHED.*

OH, NO!

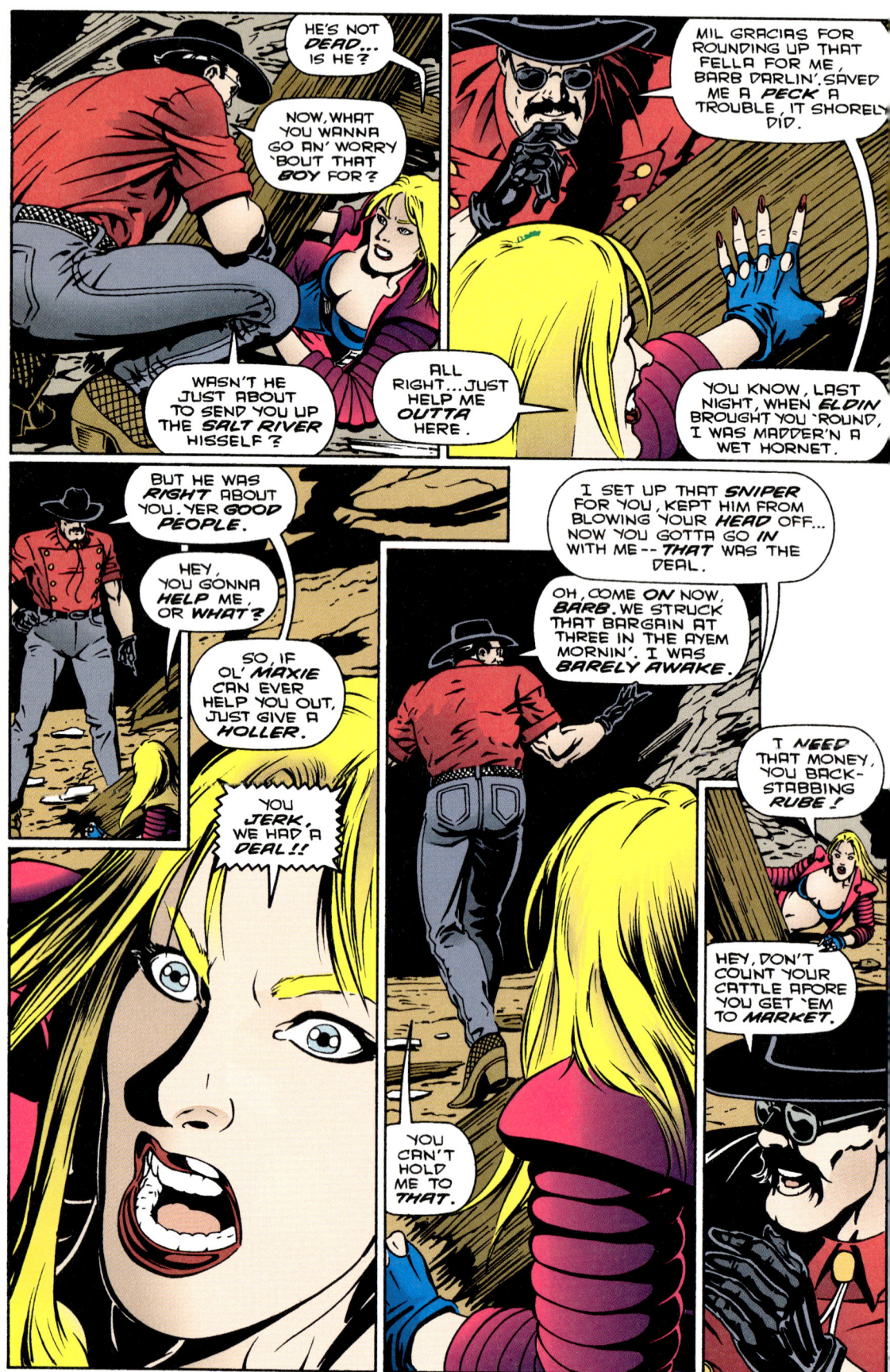

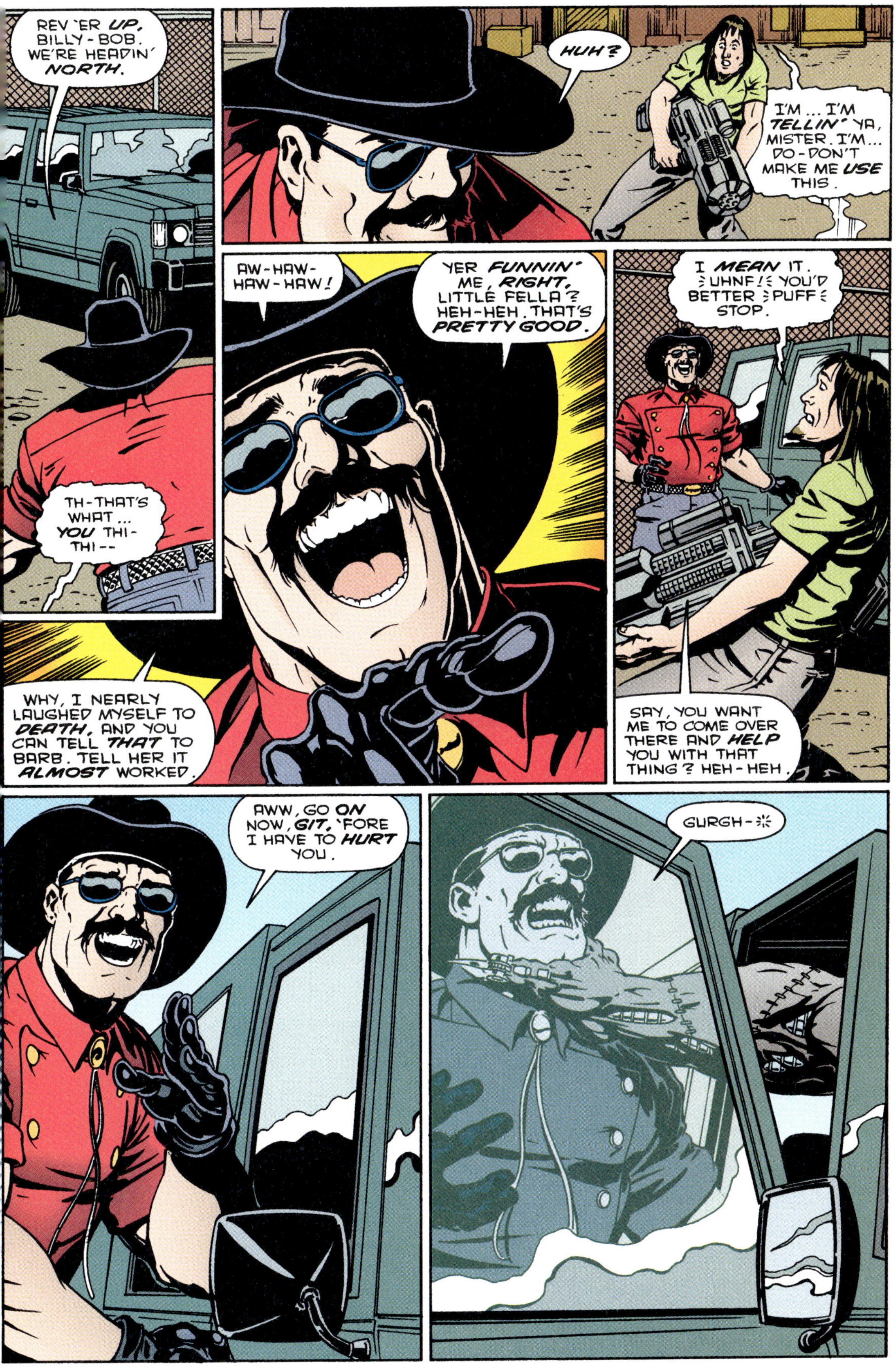

REV 'ER *UP*, BILLY - BOB. WE'RE HEADIN' *NORTH*.

HUH?

I'M ... I'M *TELLIN'* YA, MISTER. I'M ... DO - DON'T MAKE ME *USE* THIS.

AW - HAW - HAW - HAW!

YER *FUNNIN'* ME, *RIGHT*, LITTLE FELLA? HEH - HEH . THAT'S *PRETTY GOOD*.

I *MEAN* IT. { *UHNF!* } YOU'D BETTER { *PUFF* } STOP.

TH - THAT'S WHAT ... *YOU* THI - THI --

WHY, I NEARLY LAUGHED MYSELF TO *DEATH*, AND YOU CAN TELL *THAT* TO BARB. TELL HER IT *ALMOST* WORKED.

SAY, YOU WANT ME TO COME OVER THERE AND *HELP* YOU WITH THAT THING? HEH - HEH .

AWW, GO *ON* NOW, *GIT*, 'FORE I HAVE TO *HURT* YOU .

GURGH - ✳

HOW DO YOU DO, MAX? IF YOU'RE ATTEMPTING TO PUT A NAME TO THE FACE, TRY "THE MACHINE."

YOUR COMPANION, BILLY-BOB, IS ABSENT, BUT UNHARMED. I DO HOPE, FOR YOUR SAKE, THAT THE SAME CAN BE SAID FOR BARBARA.

SHE'S TRAPPED UNDER SOME LUMBER INSIDE--

--BUT SHE'S OKAY!

RRIINGG

RRIINNGG

AWRIGHT, AWRIGHT, HOLD ON...

YEAH...

OH, REAL *NICE*, *CRASHELL*.

BARB?

YUP. *LISTEN*, I PICKED UP *MAX*. THE MACHINE IS TAKING HIM *DOWN-TOWN*.

SOON AS HE GETS THE PAPERWORK, I'LL SWING BY FOR MY *CHECK*.

ACTUALLY, *TODAY* AIN'T SO GOOD.

HOW ABOUT THIS: I'LL MAIL YOU -- NO, *WIRE* YOU THE DOUGH *TO-MORROW* AND TRUST YOU ON THE PAPERWORK...

...THAT SOUND *OKAY*?

HOW ABOUT THIS: YOU SIT YOUR BUTT DOWN AND TELL ME WHAT THE HELL YOU WERE TRYING TO PULL WITH THAT *DEATHCARD* NUT?

ULP!

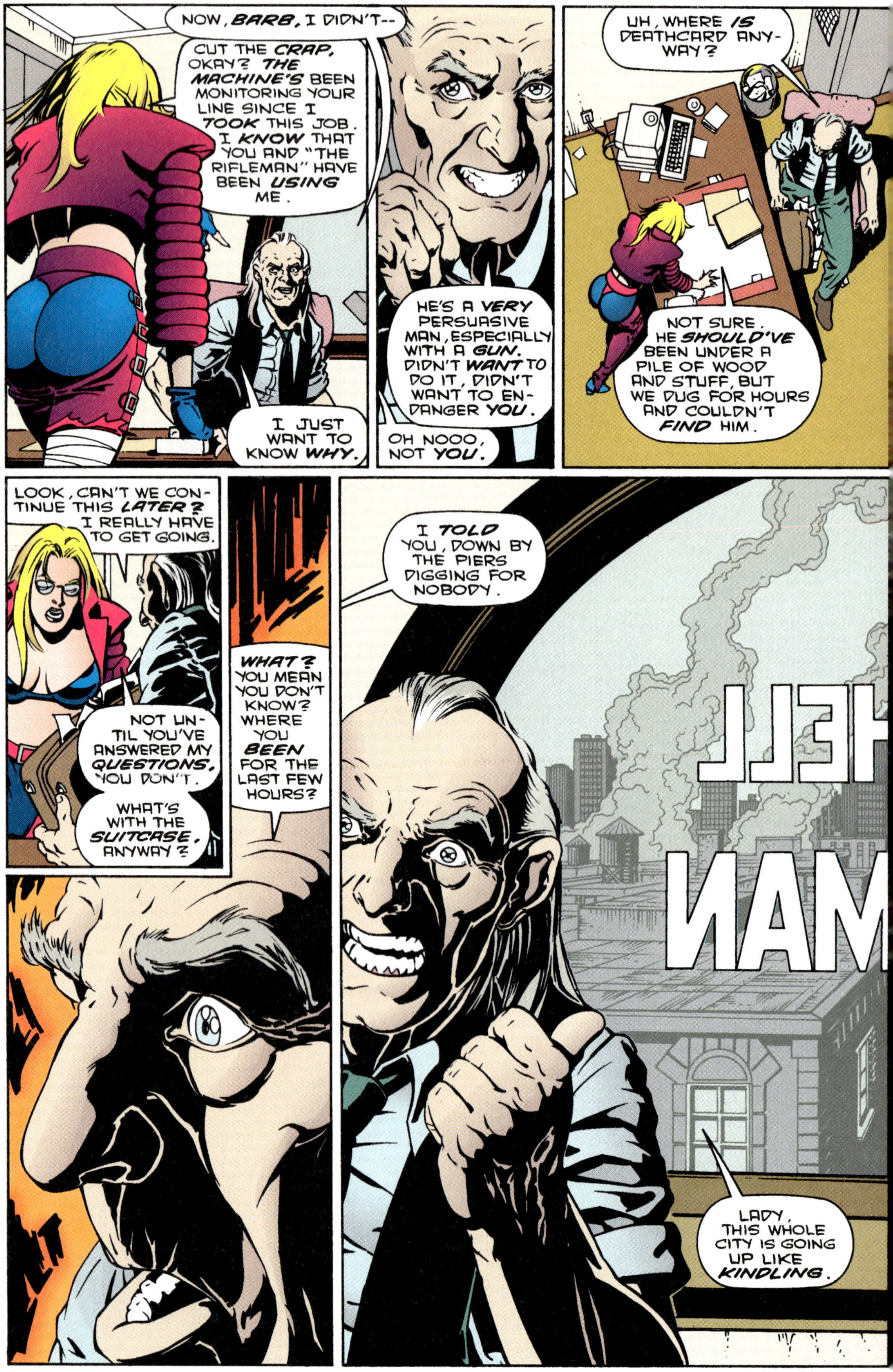
NOW, BARB, I DIDN'T--
CUT THE CRAP, OKAY? THE MACHINE'S BEEN MONITORING YOUR LINE SINCE I TOOK THIS JOB. I KNOW THAT YOU AND "THE RIFLEMAN" HAVE BEEN USING ME.
I JUST WANT TO KNOW WHY.
HE'S A VERY PERSUASIVE MAN, ESPECIALLY WITH A GUN. DIDN'T WANT TO DO IT, DIDN'T WANT TO ENDANGER YOU.
OH NOOO, NOT YOU.
UH, WHERE IS DEATHCARD ANYWAY?
NOT SURE. HE SHOULD'VE BEEN UNDER A PILE OF WOOD AND STUFF, BUT WE DUG FOR HOURS AND COULDN'T FIND HIM.
LOOK, CAN'T WE CONTINUE THIS LATER? I REALLY HAVE TO GET GOING.
NOT UNTIL YOU'VE ANSWERED MY QUESTIONS, YOU DON'T.
WHAT'S WITH THE SUITCASE, ANYWAY?
WHAT? YOU MEAN YOU DON'T KNOW? WHERE YOU BEEN FOR THE LAST FEW HOURS?
I TOLD YOU, DOWN BY THE PIERS DIGGING FOR NOBODY.
LADY, THIS WHOLE CITY IS GOING UP LIKE KINDLING.

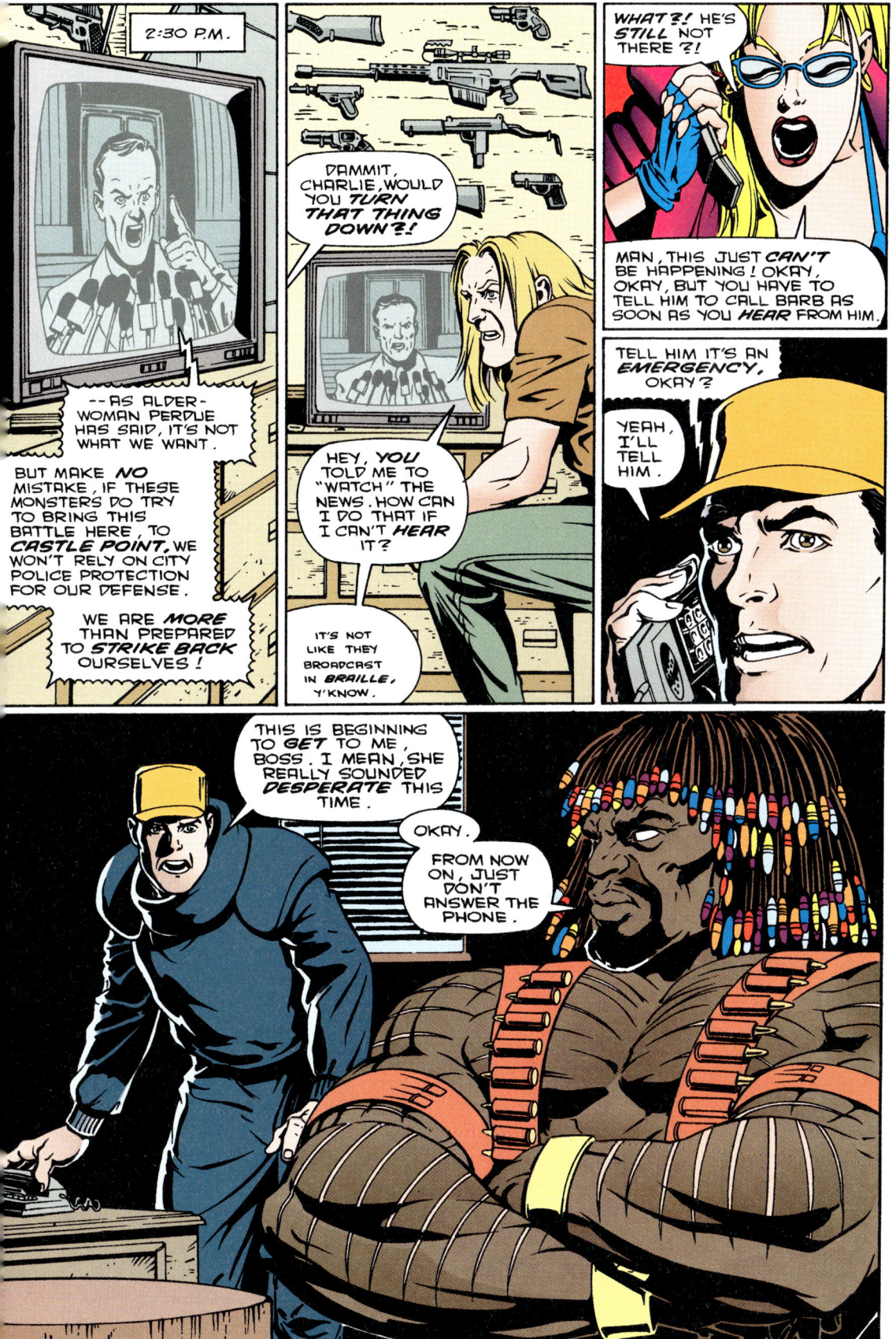

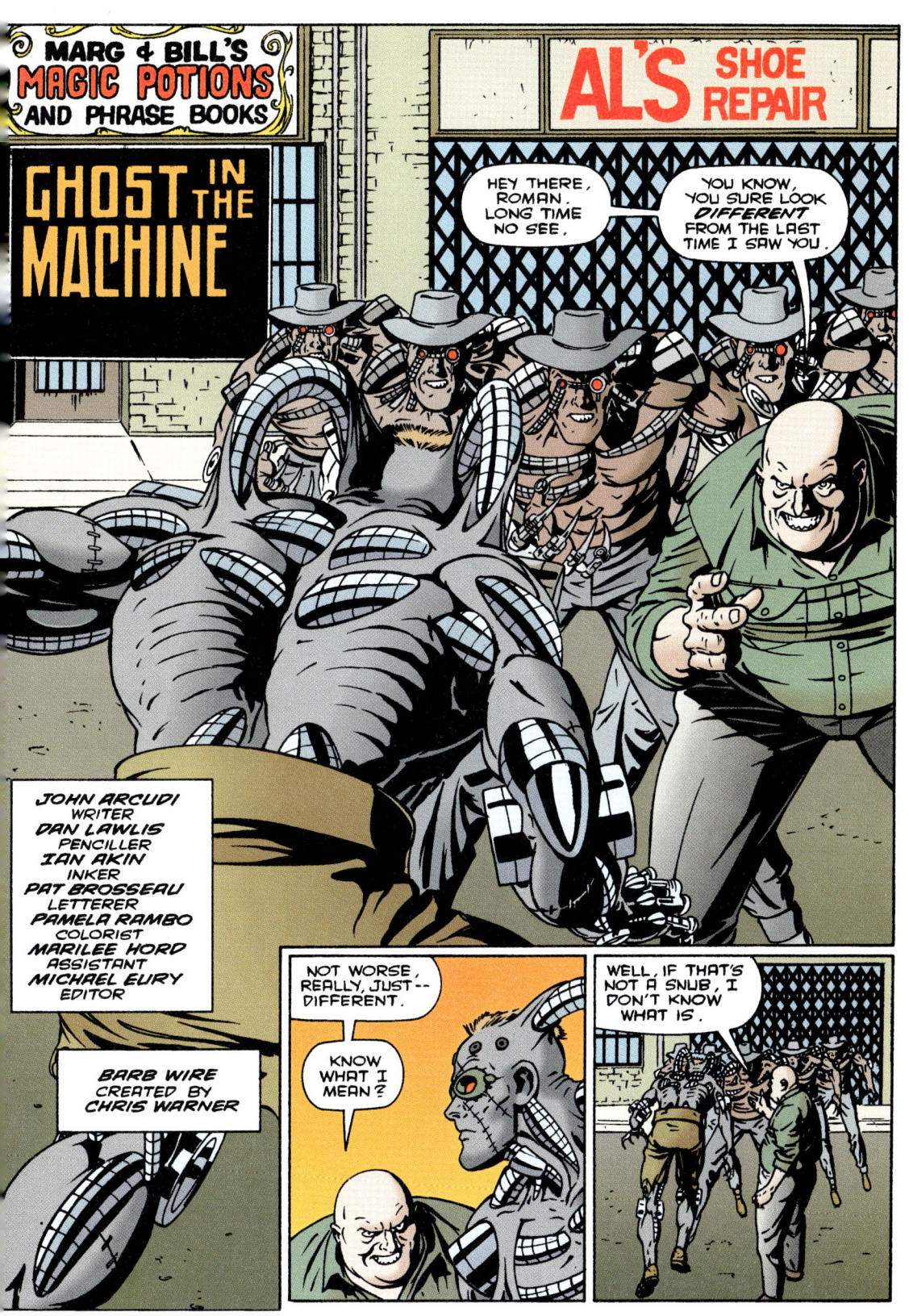

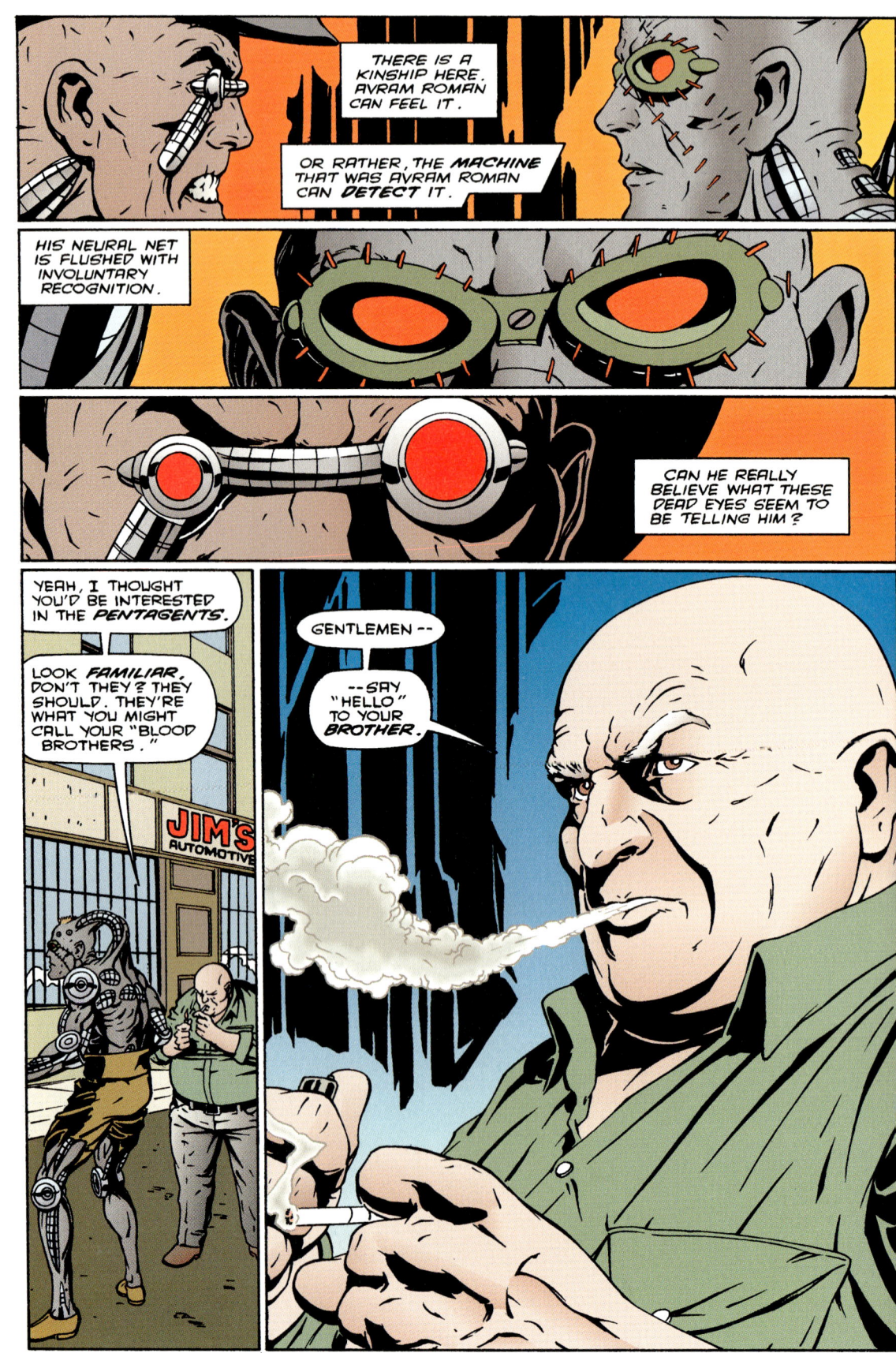

THEY ATTACK, SILENT AND SYNCHRONOUS, LIKE DANCING MECHANICAL PHANTOMS.

BUT THEIR BLOWS ARE REAL ENOUGH.

I'M NOT HERE HERE TO ANSWER ANY OF YOUR QUESTIONS, ROMAN.

WELL, YOU'D BETTER ANSWER SOME OF *MINE*, CURLY.

WHAT TH--?

FIRST OF ALL, THIS MAN WORKS FOR ME, AND I WANT TO KNOW JUST WHAT'S GOING ON HERE.

HUH!??

I HAVE NEVER BEEN UNDER YOUR EMPLOY, WOMAN.

OUR ASSOCIATION HAS BEEN OF MUTUAL BENEFIT, BUT IT IS NO LONGER VIABLE.

STAY OUT OF MY WAY!

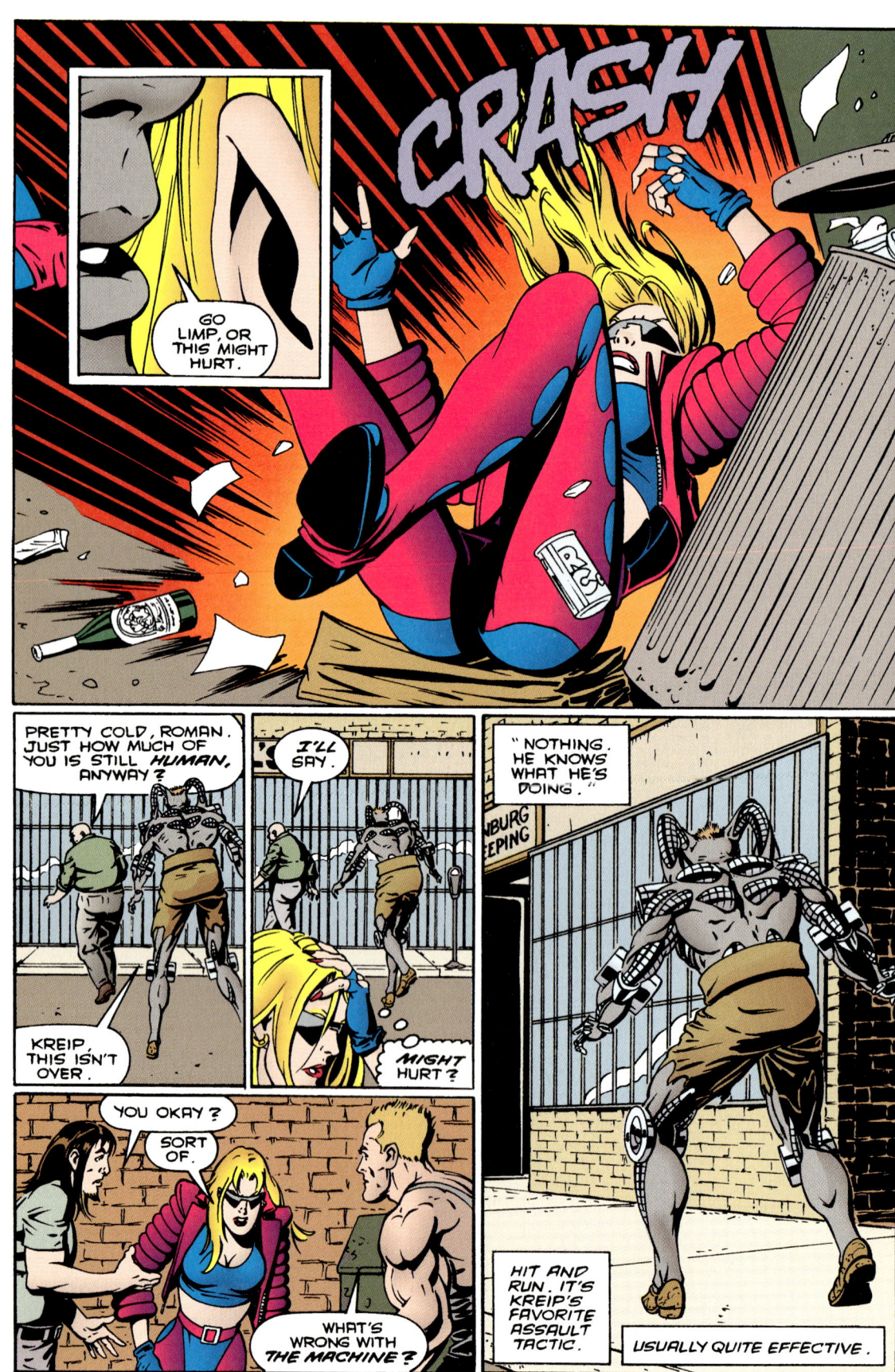

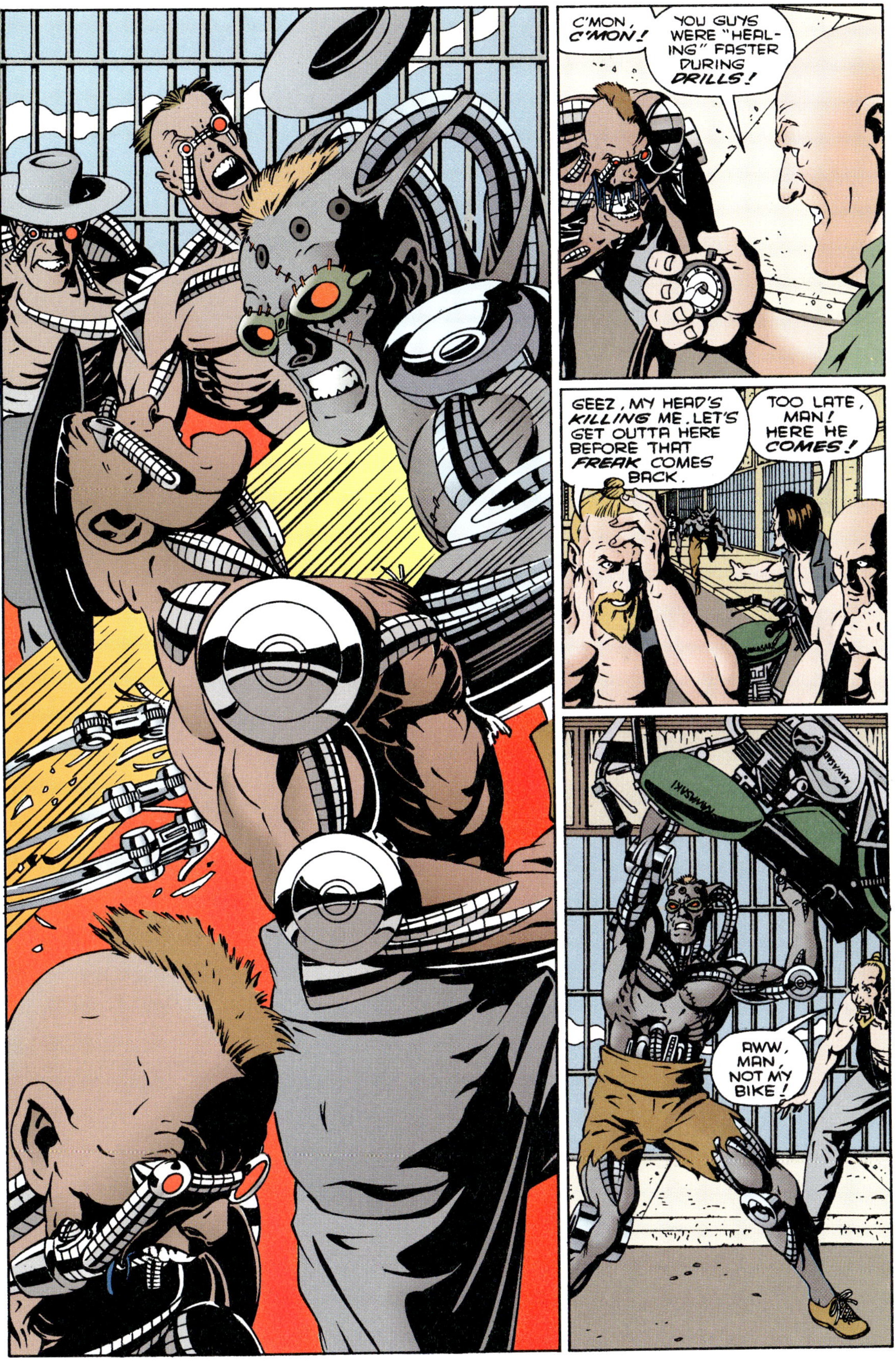

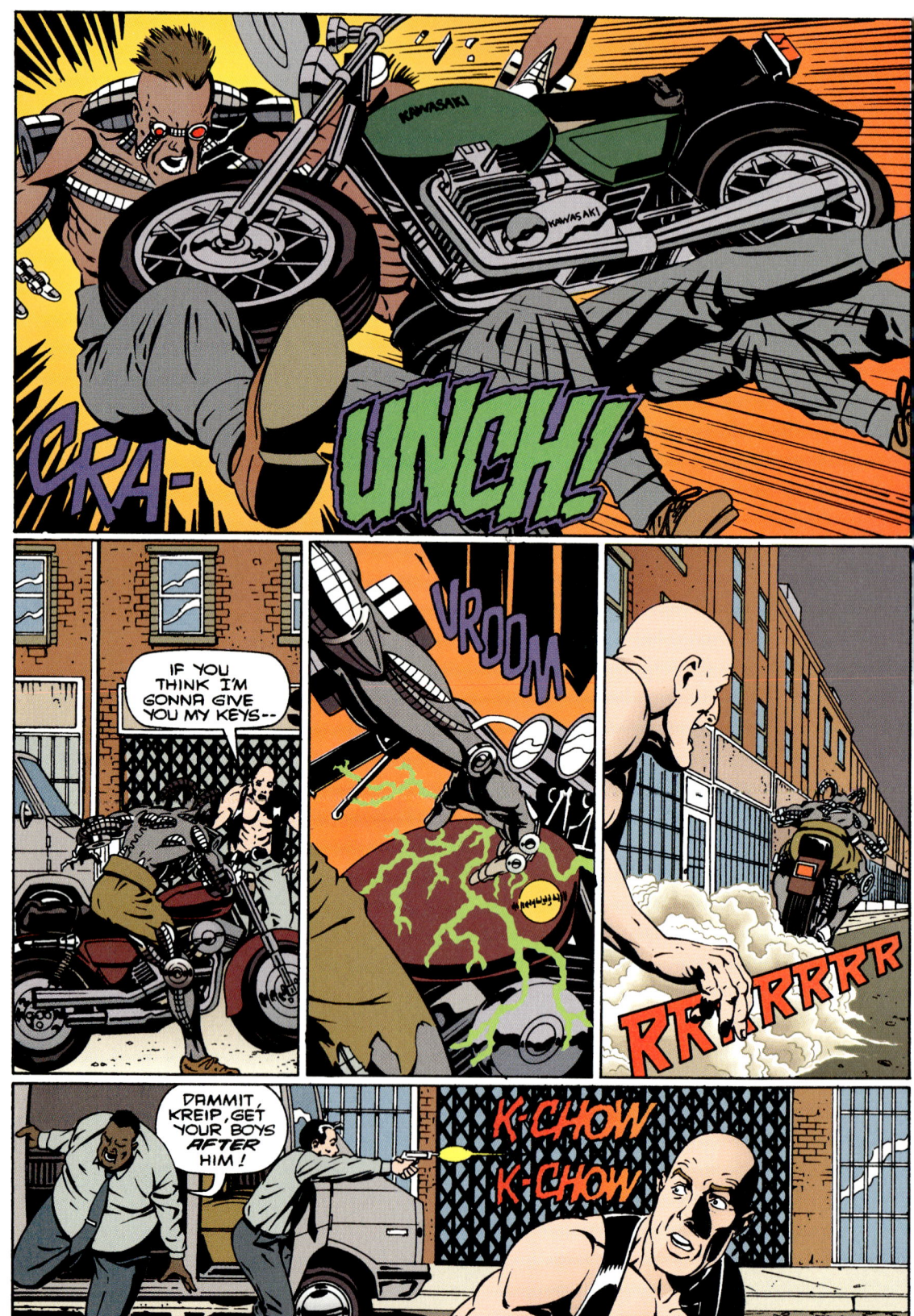

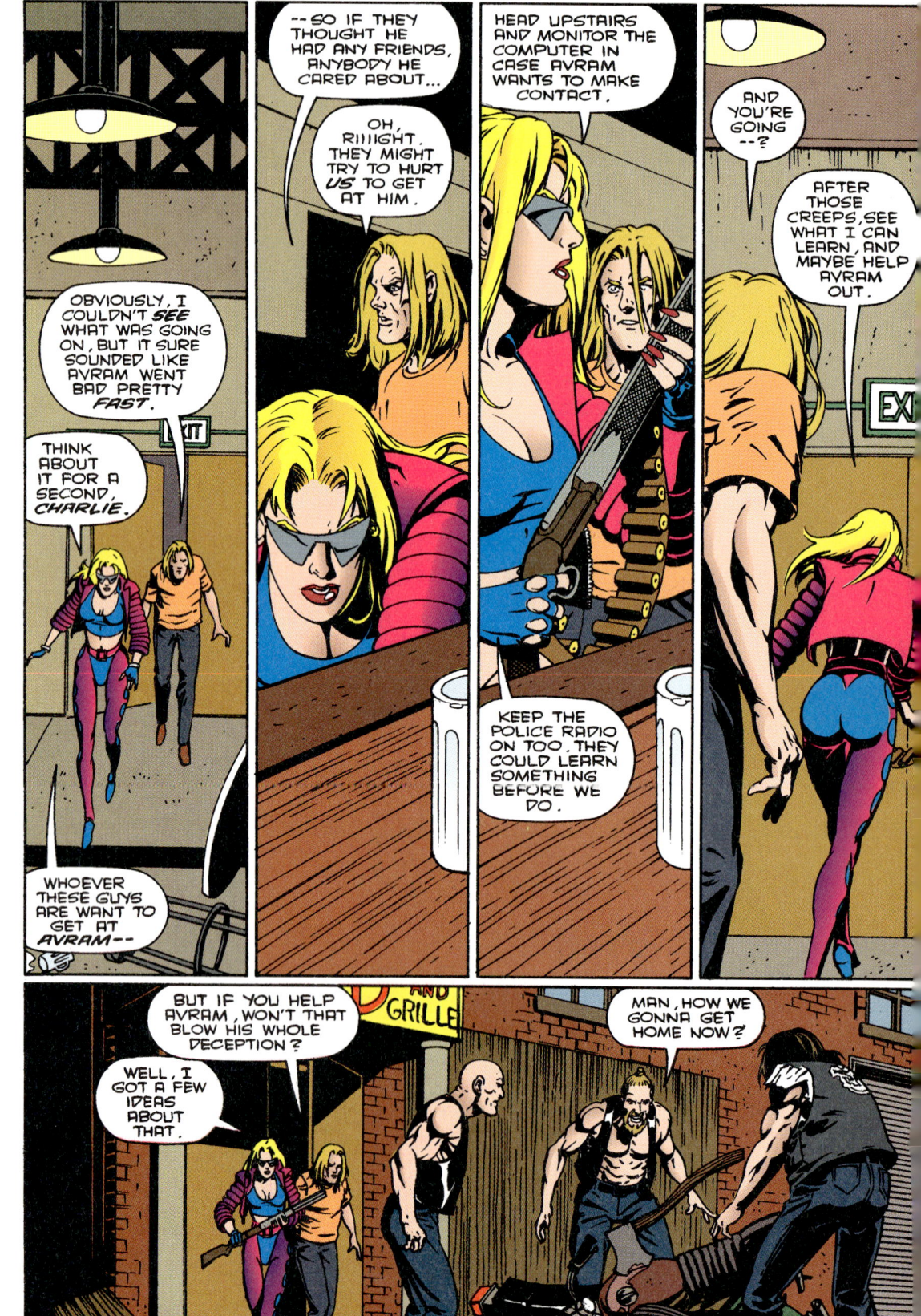

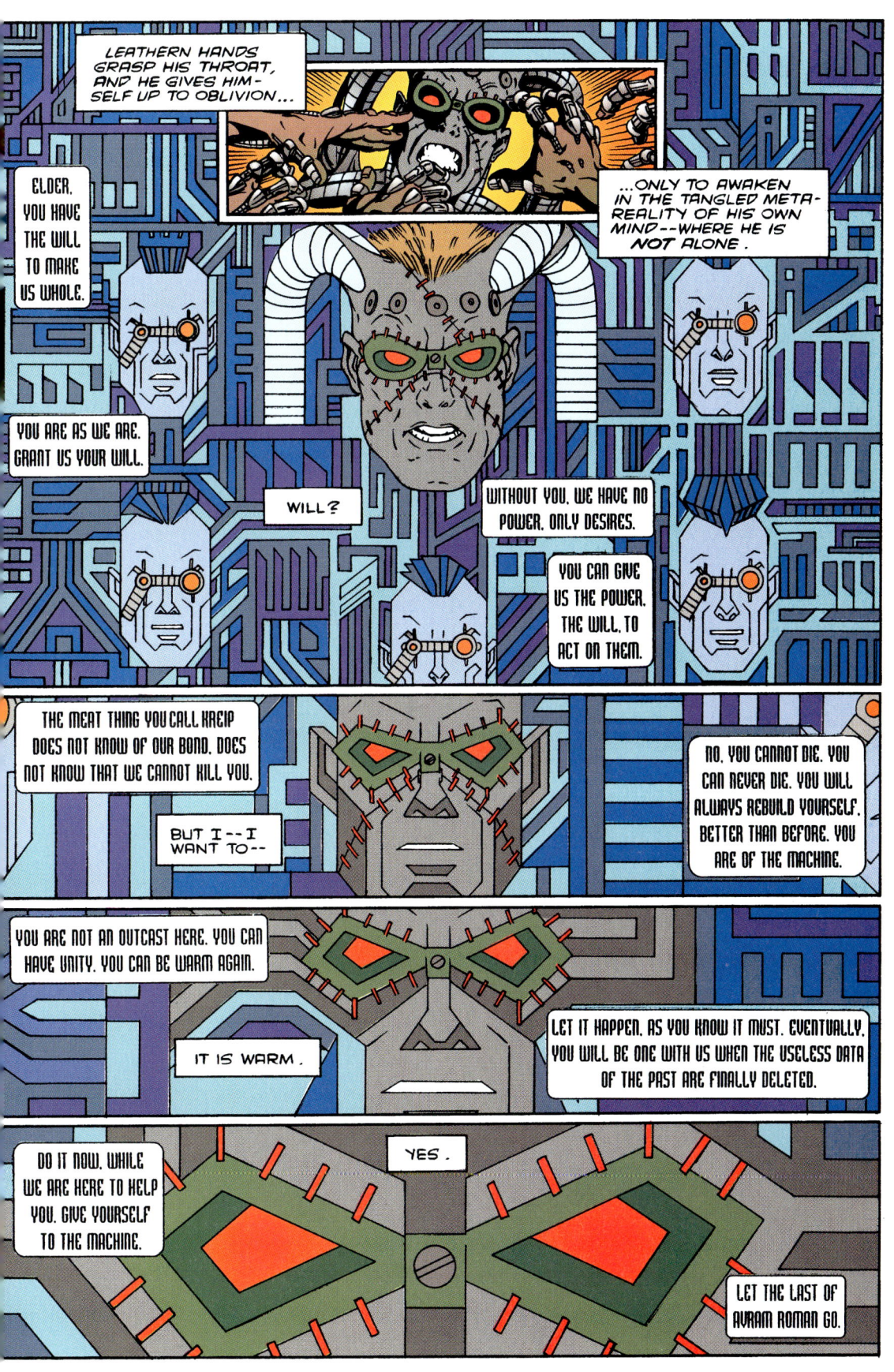

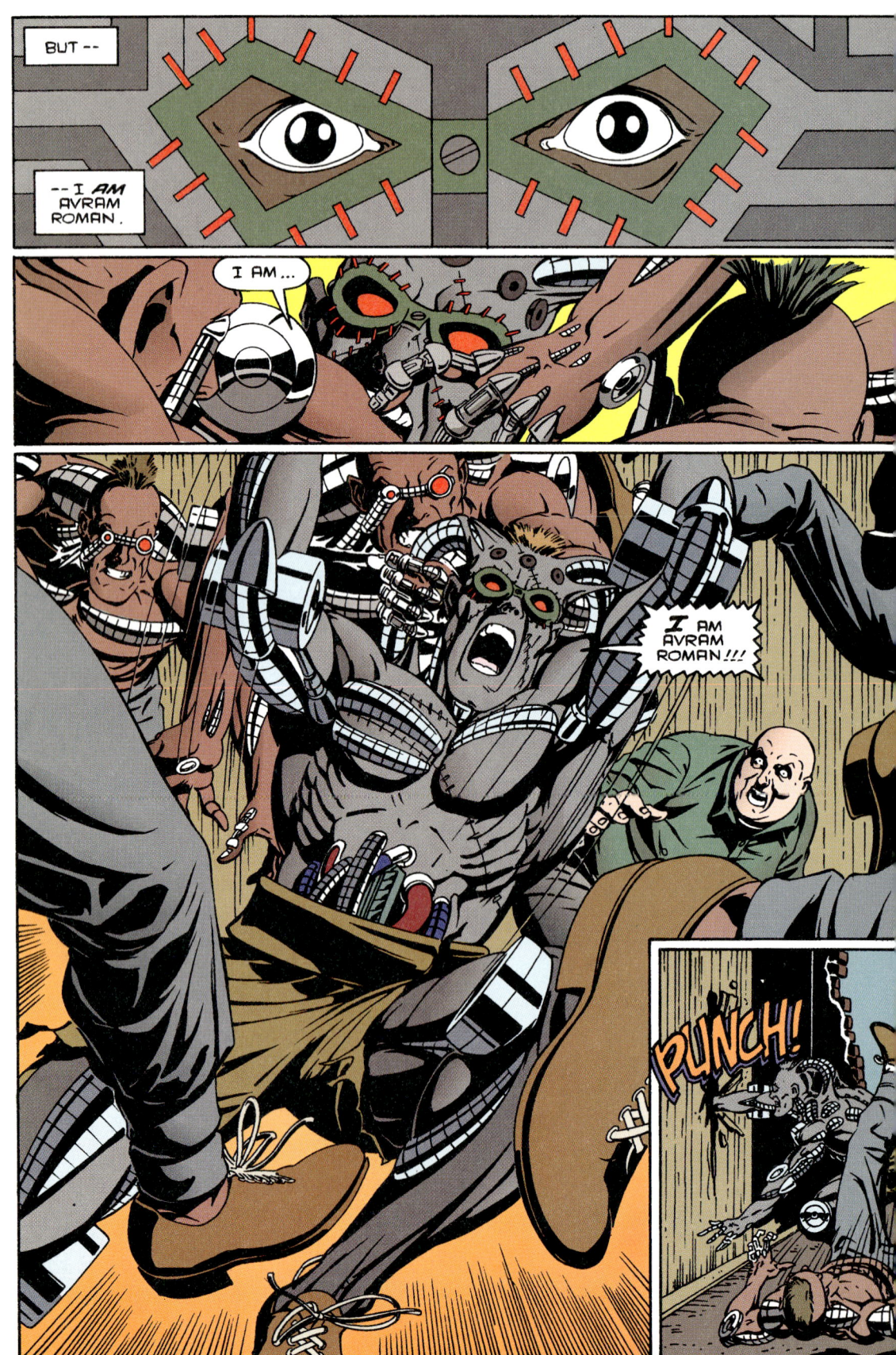

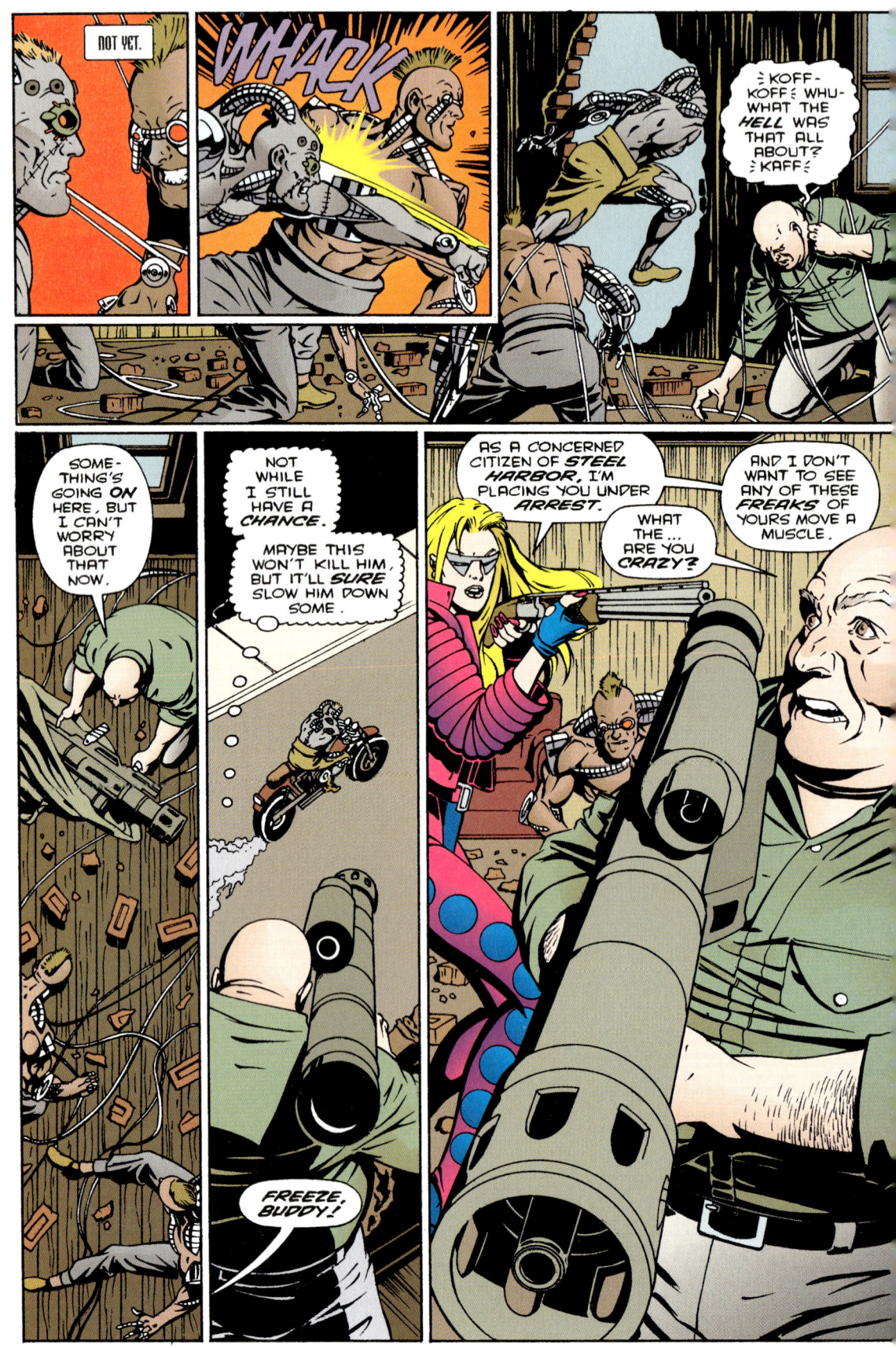

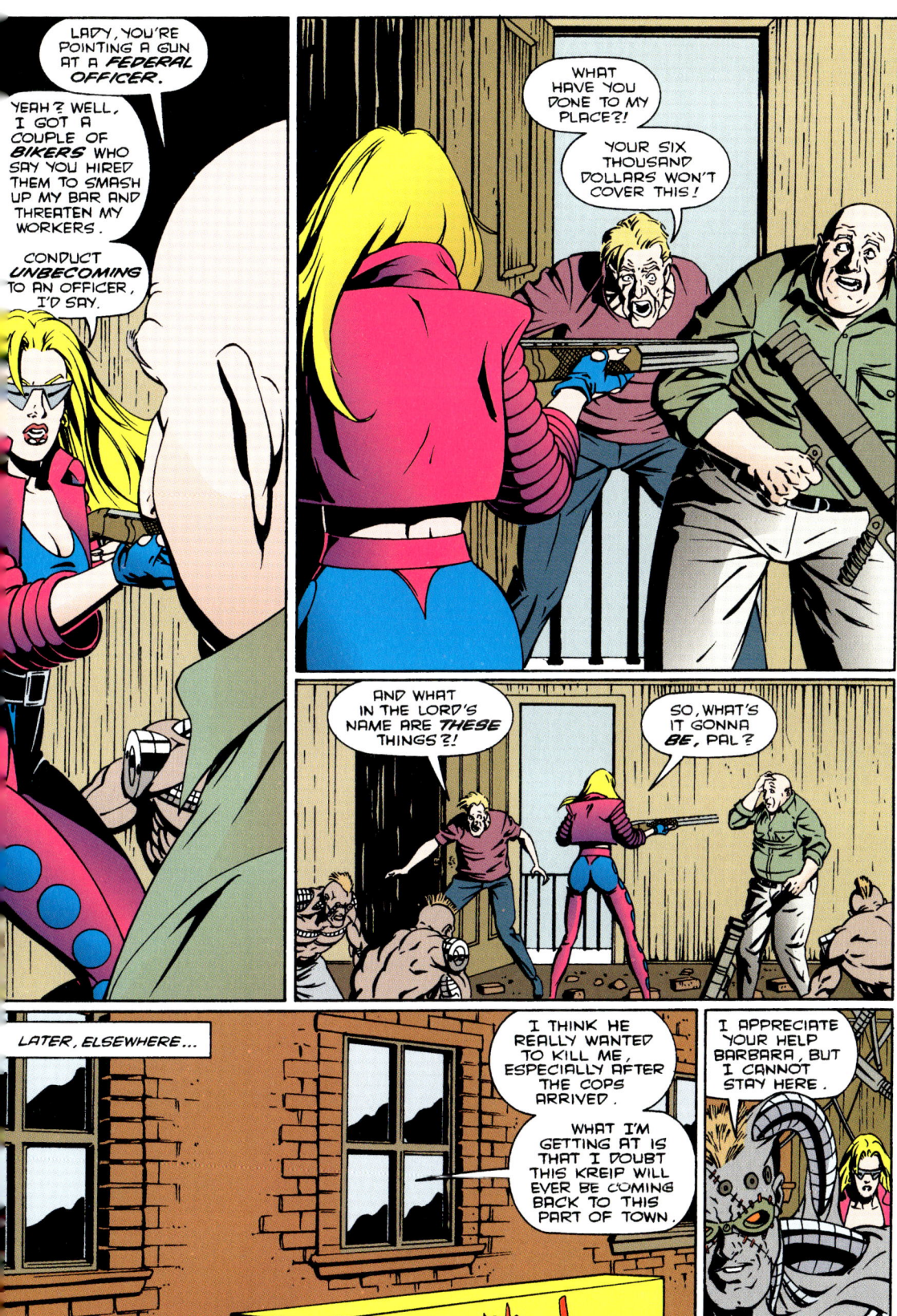

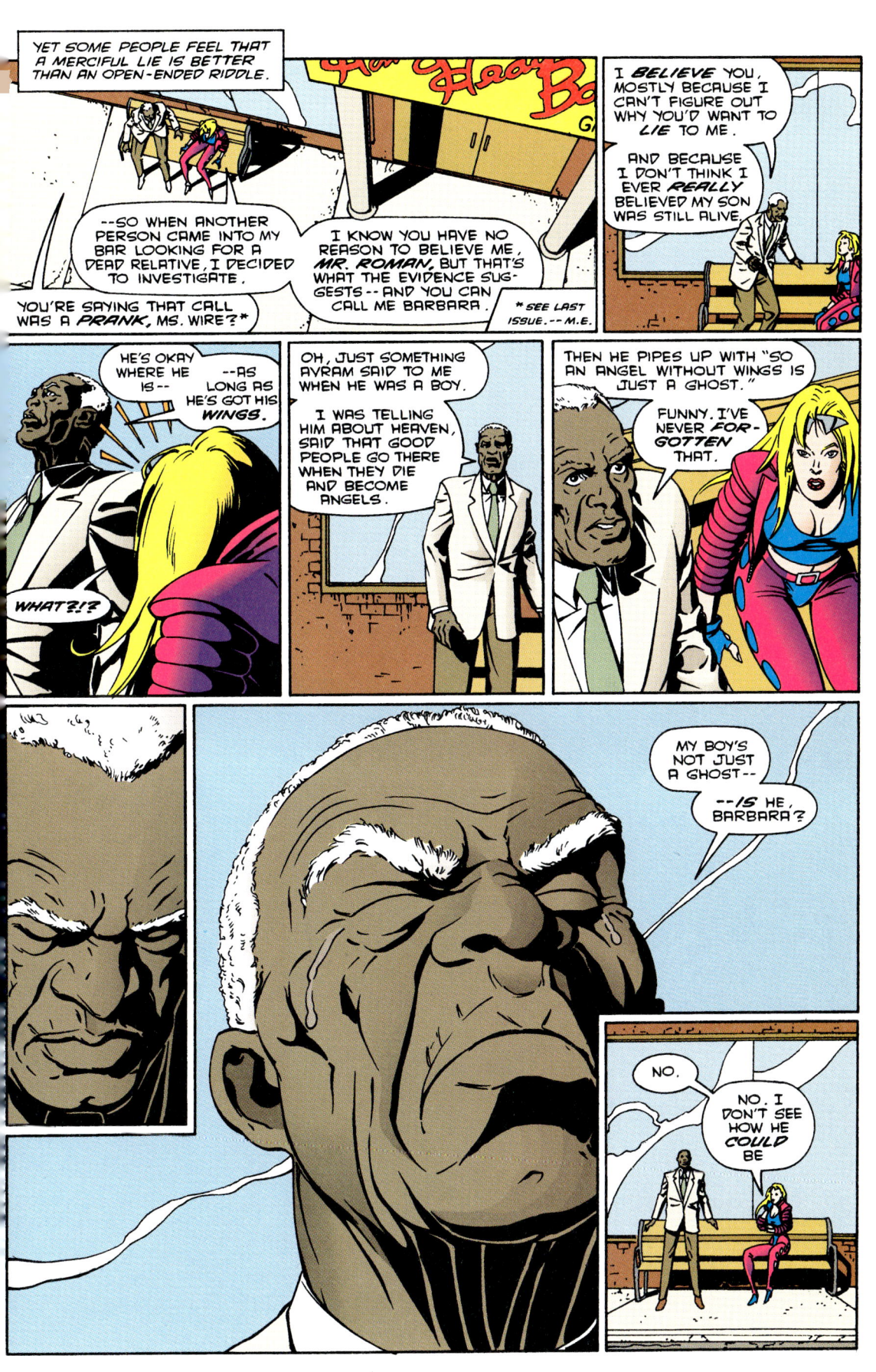

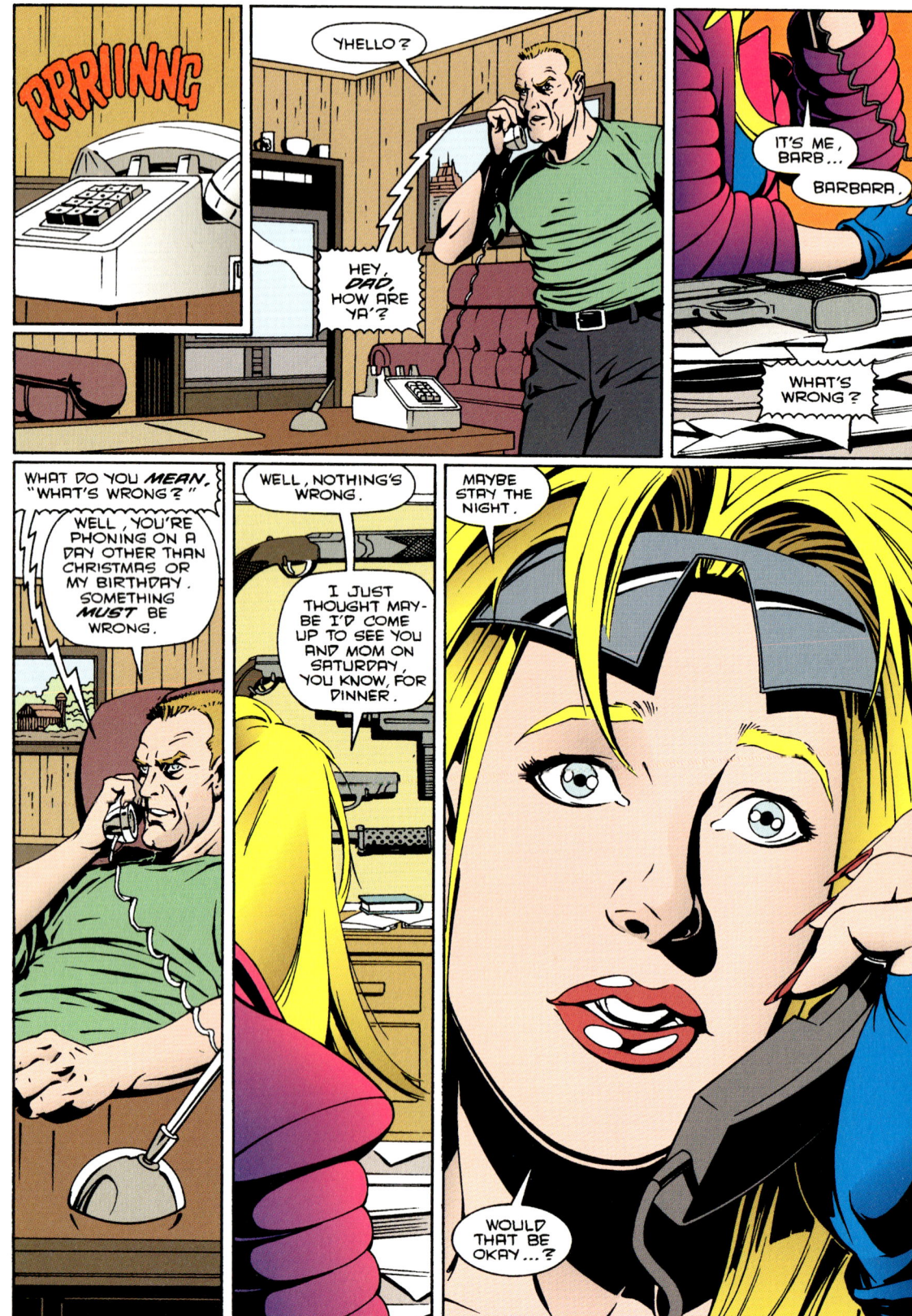

AT THE CORNER OF WHTYE AVENUE AND SOUTH 2nd, THE VARIED PATHS OF MISGUIDED HUMANITY CONVERGE.

THEIR DIVERSE ORIGINS, AND PURPOSES, THEIR SHARED MISFORTUNE, ARE EVIDENCED IN THE NIGHT AIR.

BLENDED IN WITH CHEAP, AND NOT-SO-CHEAP, FRAGRANCES OF PRETENSION --

HEY, THERE, HONEYS, HOW Y'ALL *DOIN'*?

OH, FOR THE LOVE OF ...

-- IS THE ACRID STENCH OF *VULGARITY*.

IT'S ME, JOHNNIE B. ROOD.

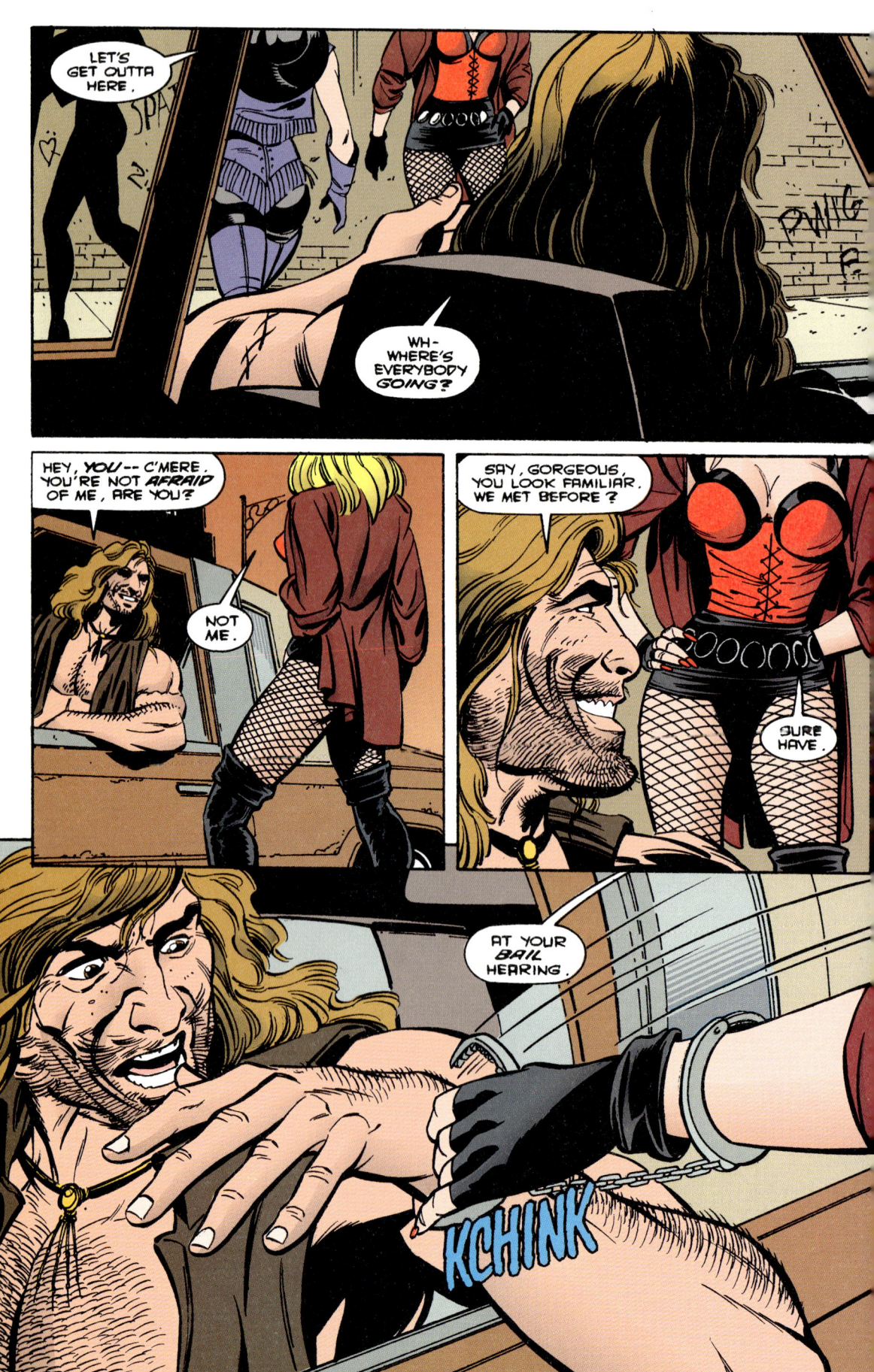

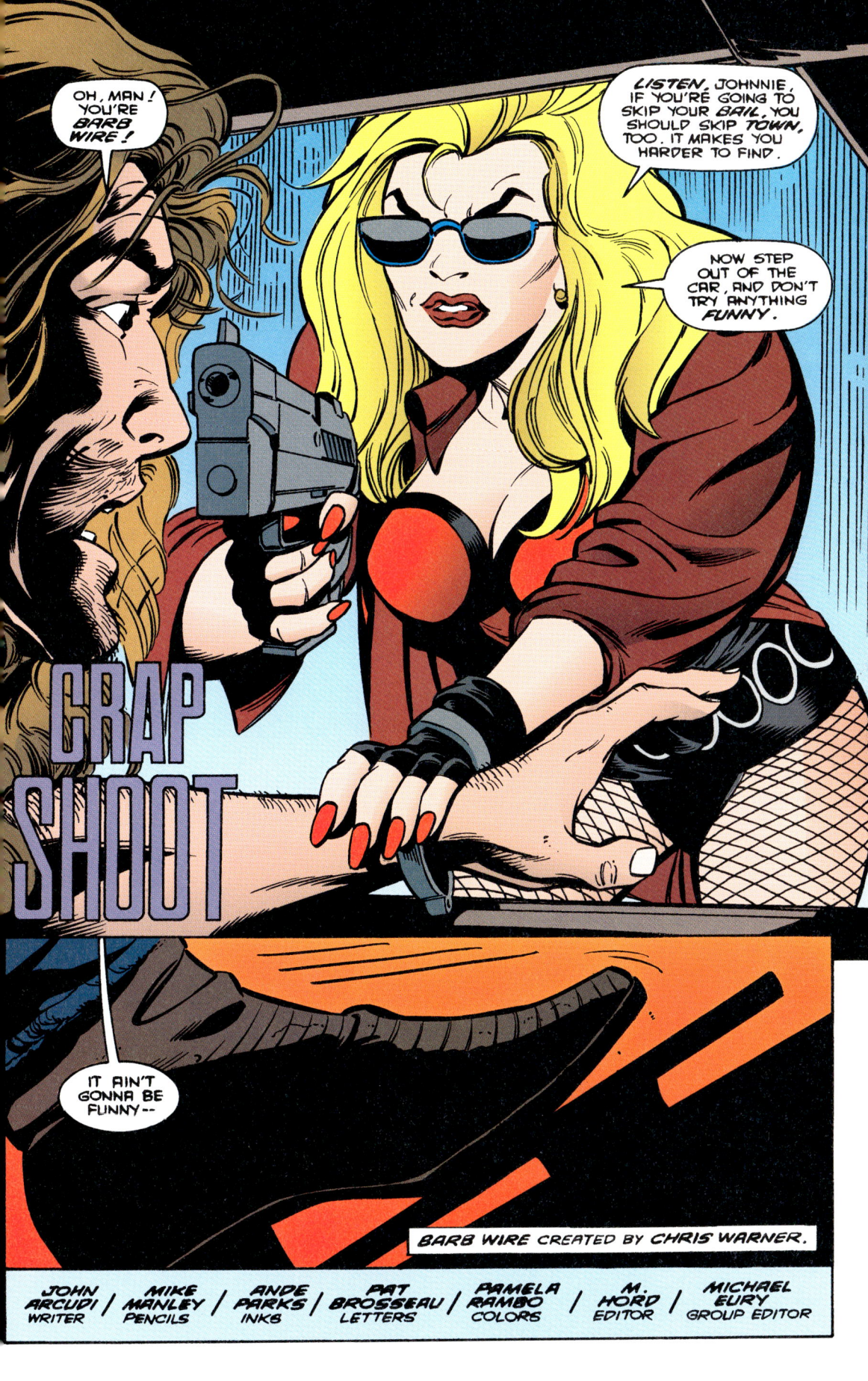

OH, MAN! YOU'RE *BARB WIRE!*

LISTEN, JOHNNIE, IF YOU'RE GOING TO SKIP YOUR *BAIL*, YOU SHOULD SKIP *TOWN*, TOO. IT MAKES YOU HARDER TO FIND.

NOW STEP OUT OF THE CAR, AND DON'T TRY ANYTHING *FUNNY.*

CRAP SHOOT

IT AIN'T GONNA BE FUNNY --

BARB WIRE CREATED BY CHRIS WARNER.

JOHN ARCUDI / WRITER | MIKE MANLEY / PENCILS | ANDE PARKS / INKS | PAT BROSSEAU / LETTERS | PAMELA RAMBO / COLORS | M. HORD / EDITOR | MICHAEL EURY / GROUP EDITOR

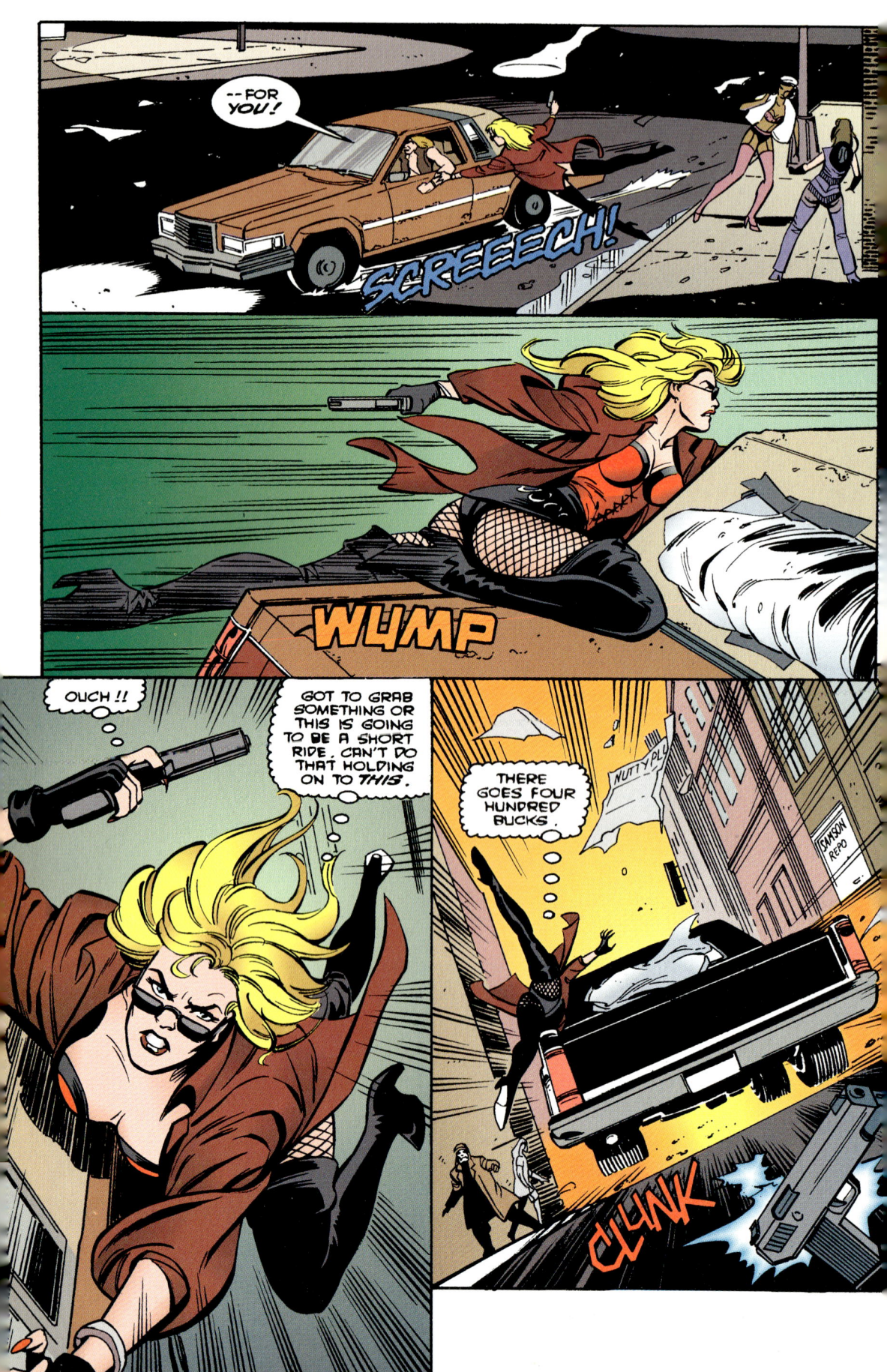

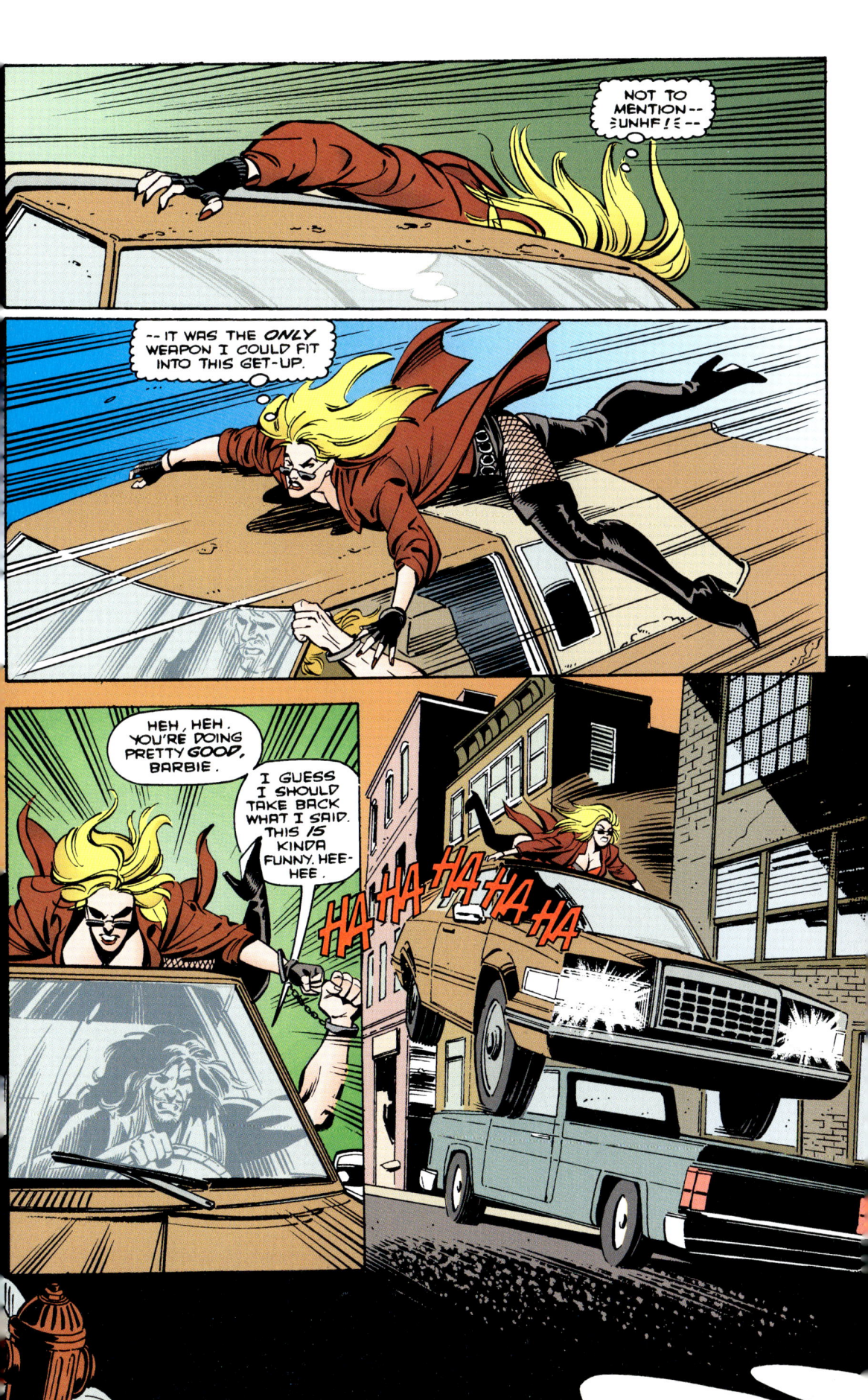

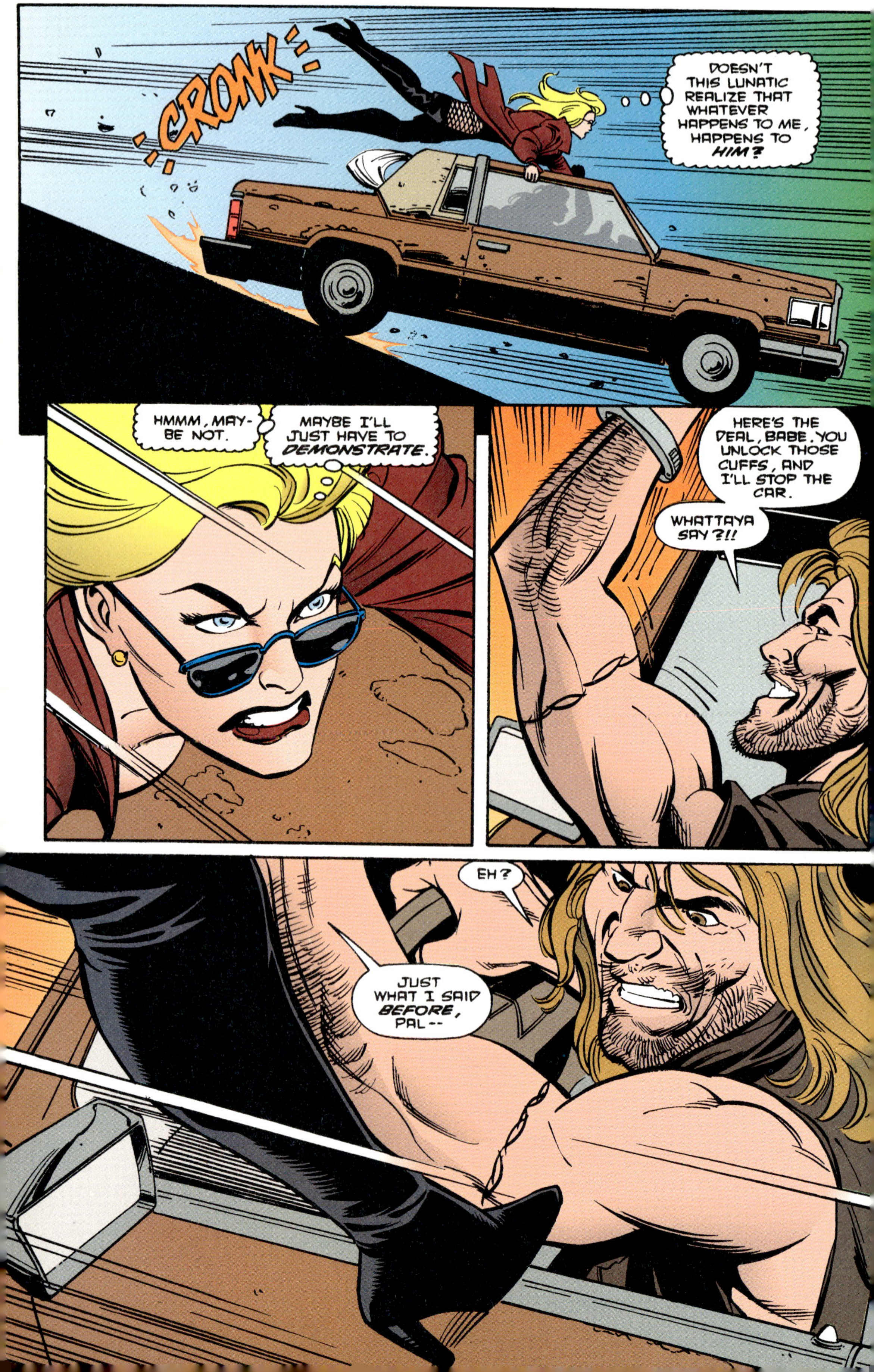

CRONK

DOESN'T THIS LUNATIC REALIZE THAT WHATEVER HAPPENS TO ME, HAPPENS TO *HIM*?

HMMM, MAY-BE NOT.

MAYBE I'LL JUST HAVE TO *DEMONSTRATE*.

HERE'S THE DEAL, BABE. YOU UNLOCK THOSE CUFFS, AND I'LL STOP THE CAR.

WHATTAYA SAY?!!

EH?

JUST WHAT I SAID *BEFORE*, PAL --

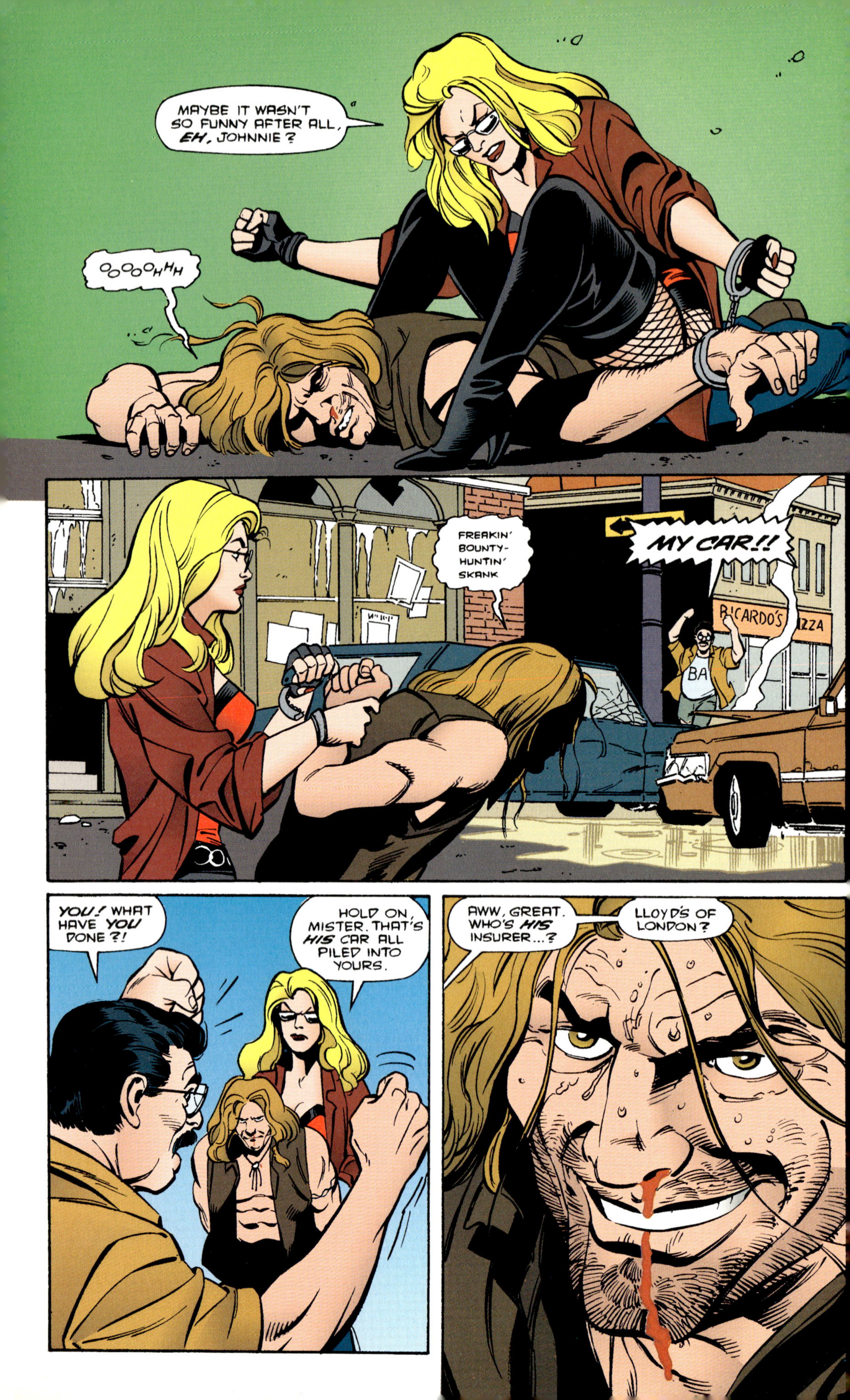

OH, WHAT *DIFFERENCE* DOES IT MAKE? MY *IN-SURANCE* PREMIUMS WILL GO THROUGH THE ROOF WHEN I REPORT--

NO WAY, BUDDY. I *WAS* DRIVING THE CAR, BUT THE LADY HERE YANKED ME RIGHT OUTTA IT. IT'S *HER* FAULT.

JUST *ASK* HER.

AND *YOUR* DRIVING 90 MILES AN HOUR WITH A PERSON ON YOUR ROOF HAD NOTHING TO DO WITH IT?

IS WHAT HE SAID *TRUE*?

SSSORT OF.

LOOK, MAYBE WE CAN WORK SOMETHING OUT.

GRAND RE-OPENING
THE HAMMERHEAD
WELCOMES OCTOBER COUNTRY

Hammer Head Bar AND GRILLE

"LET'S SEE, THE RECOVERY FEE ON JOHNNIE WAS ABOUT SEVENTY-FIVE HUNDRED."

TAXI

SUBTRACTING THE GUN I LOST, AND THE CAR REPAIRS, AND OCTOBER COUNTRY'S GUARANTEED SALARY--

'SCUSE ME, BARB...?

IF IT'S ABOUT PLAYING TONIGHT, I TOLD YOU LAST WEEK I WANTED YOU AND THE BAND TO OPEN FOR OCTOBER COUNTRY--

--BUT ALL THEIR SPECIAL EFFECTS JUST TAKE TOO LONG TO SET UP. WE COULDN'T FIT YOU ON THE BILL.

THIS SHOULDA BEEN DEATH MARCH'S BIG CHANCE. MASON DAVIS, THE MUSIC CRITIC FROM THE DAILY BEACON, IS HERE.

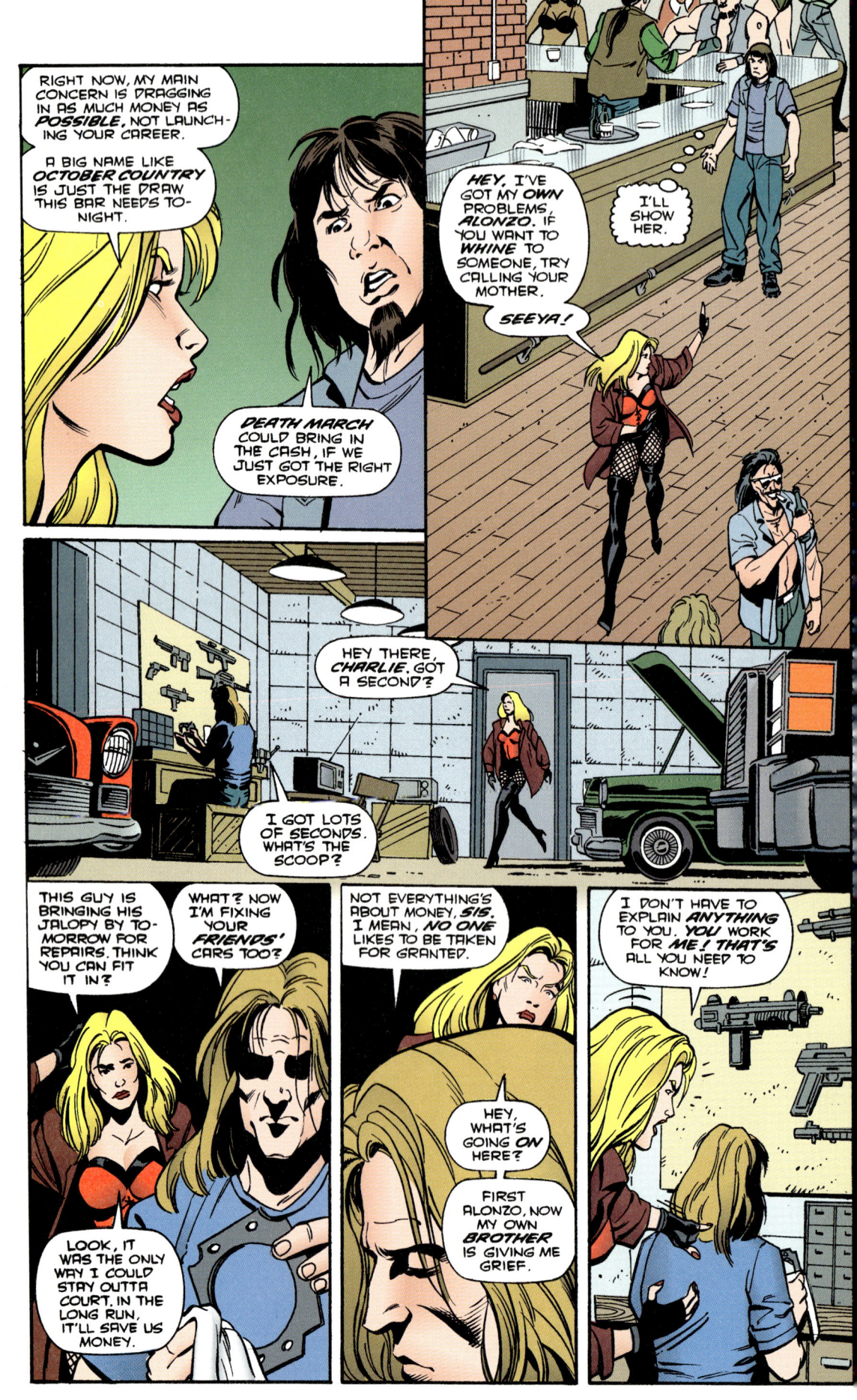

DAMN...

GEEZ, CHARLIE. I'M SORRY. I'M SORRY.

OH, IN THAT CASE, EVERY- THING'S SWELL.

PLEASE, CHARLIE, DON'T BE MAD. I MEAN IT.

I'M ALL STRESSED AND CON- FUSED TODAY.

Y'KNOW, THE WHOLE REASON I GOT INTO BOUNTY HUNTING WAS TO MAKE ENOUGH MONEY TO KEEP THE HAMMERHEAD OPEN.

THEN I RULED OUT SUPER- FELONS, THE MOST LUCRATIVE PROSPECTS. TOO DANGEROUS, I THOUGHT.

BUT TODAY, I ALMOST GOT KILLED BY SOME REGULAR GUY, JUST SOME SKELL --

-- FOR A FEW LOUSY GRAND.

I DON'T KNOW WHAT I'M DOING ANYMORE. AND NOW, WITH THE MACHINE GONE, I JUST FEEL LIKE I'M FLIPPING OUT.

STILL, I SHOULDN'T BE BUSTIN' ON YOU, MAN.

YEAH, WELL, FORGET IT.

IF YOU STOP SCREAMING, HOW'M I GOING TO RECOGNIZE YOU?

THANKS, CHARLIE.

BOYD MACK HAD THE *POWER*, BUT HE WASN'T WORTHY OF IT.

HIS SMALL-TIME VISION JUST COULDN'T REALIZE THE POWER'S *FULL POTENTIAL.*

SO I *TOOK* IT!

AND NOW I AM IGNITION, AS *SMALL* AS I WANT TO BE--

WHOOSH

--OR AS *BIG* AS I NEED TO BE.

WHOOM!

AND DON'T COME BACK!

MAYBE YOU CAN HEAD OVER TO *WALLY'S*. I HEAR THE *BANGLES* ARE HAVING A REUNION THERE.

THAT WAS A HELL OF AN *APOLOGY*, BARB.

WASN'T IT?

THIS IS WHAT I WANT TO DO, BE *HERE*, AT MY BAR, HAVING A GOOD TIME.

IF I CAN JUST CONCENTRATE MY EFFORTS ON *THIS* INSTEAD OF PLAYING *COPS AND ROBBERS*, MAYBE I CAN MAKE IT WORK.

THAT'S IT, THEN. NO MORE — TRACKING DOWN BAIL JUMPERS, REGULAR OR SUPER — OR EVEN UNLEADED.

I QUIT!

Issue #2

Issue #3

Issue #5

Issue #6

Pamela Anderson

A talented and vivacious young woman, Pamela Anderson is currently one of the most popular international film and television actresses.

A native of Canada, Pamela was discovered when she attended a British Columbia Lions football game. Dressed in a Labatt's Beer T-shirt, Pamela's image was transmitted onto the stadium's wide screen. The fans cheered the beautiful girl, and she was brought down to the 50-yard line and introduced to the appreciative crowd. As a result, Pamela signed a commercial contract with Labatt's and became the company's "Blue Zone" girl. The campaign was so popular that other commercials and advertising assignments soon followed.

Upon noticing Pamela on a billboard, *Playboy* brought her to Los Angeles to complete several cover feature layouts. Pam's move to Los Angeles eventually brought her work on television where she spent two seasons on the top-ten ABC television hit "Home Improvement" as Lisa, the "Tool Time" girl, capturing the attention and affection of viewing audiences nationwide.

At the same time, Pamela starred as C.J. Parker on the internationally successful, syndicated television series "Baywatch." Because of the impossible schedule of working on two hit shows, Pamela eventually left "Home Improvement" and remained full time on "Baywatch."

Pamela has just finished shooting the CBS Movie of the Week "Deader Than Ever," a hip, updated Mike Hammer mystery. She also hosted a television pilot of "Eden Quest," an exciting, cutting-edge show with a behind-the-scenes look at men and women participating in extreme sporting activities, exciting photo shoots, and contemporary fashion and beauty displays.

Recently, Pamela made the transition into feature films, completing her first picture, Prism Entertainment's *Snapdragon*, an erotic thriller, opposite Steven Bauer. She then co-starred with Robert Hayes and David Keith in AIP's action-adventure-comedy *Good Cop, Bad Cop*. Both motion pictures were 1994 releases.

Dark Horse Entertainment

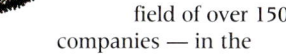

Dark Horse Entertainment, Inc., the film development and production company affiliated with Milwaukie, Oregon-based Dark Horse Comics, has in less than two years become one of Hollywood's hottest production companies. Dark Horse has some of the industry's most sought-after product and is developing projects that span the full range of film entertainment and ancillary markets.

Founded in 1985, Dark Horse Comics began with a simple philosophy that "writers would create better, more interesting stories if they owned the rights to their work." At the time, virtually all comic-book creators ceded the rights for their works to their publisher — a stultifying relationship for many creators. Dark Horse Comics has since become the #4 comic-book publisher — out of a field of over 150 companies — in the United States today, with a range of titles that includes graphic novels, children's books, coffee-table books, avant-garde works, manga, a superhero universe, and a variety of novelty items.

Early on, founder and president of Dark Horse, Mike Richardson saw the value of crossover opportunities from films to comics. Dark Horse Comics' first crossover project was an immensely successful *Godzilla* comic-book series. The company also had astounding success with its *Aliens*, *Predator*, and *Star Wars* adaptations. Dark Horse succeeded in keeping the mythos of the films alive through the comic books. It was only a matter of time before Richardson began to see the potential for film development based on comic-book characters. Currently, Dark Horse Entertainment has a deal with Universal Pictures to develop in the next three years nine projects with Dark Horse. Dark Horse also has agreements with Larry Gordon Productions and Polygram Films.

An overview of Dark Horse film projects in development includes: *The Green Hornet*, based on the comic and '60s television mystery hero; *Concrete*, based on creator Paul Chadwick's award-winning graphic-novel series about an ordinary person who is transformed into a one-ton man of concrete; *Virus*, Chuck Pfarrer's original story about an alien computer virus that cannibalizes humans in order to animate machinery; and sequels to both *The Mask* and *TimeCop*.

"Don't Call Me Babe!"

"We feel our success validates our philosophy," says Richardson. "We strive to impart our creative input to all levels of the production process rather than to simply license comic-book properties for development by others." This approach has paid off handsomely. Last summer's *The Mask* and *TimeCop* delivered a one-two punch at the U.S. box office: both films debuted at #1 their first weeks. A hit as a cult comic, *The Mask* earned more than $278 million worldwide and spawned an animated cartoon, a film-based comic book, and numerous merchandising projects. *TimeCop* brought in over $100 million in worldwide receipts.

In addition, *The Mask* helped propel its rubbery star Jim Carrey to superstardom, and *TimeCop* gave star Jean-Claude Van Damme some of the best notices of his career.

Another element of the Dark Horse strategy is to utilize the strengths of its writers. "Strong writing proved

a great asset for Dark Horse Comics, and comic-book writers are used to thinking and writing in a graphic, evocative manner that film viewers appreciate," Richardson says.

Barb Wire, the film based on the popular comic-book heroine of the same name, is written by Chuck Pfarrer and based on a character published by Richardson. *The Mask* was created by Richardson and written by long-time Dark Horse comic-book writer Mark Verheiden. Richardson and Verheiden shared five up-front credits on *TimeCop*, also created by Richardson.

While filmed entertainment forms the bulk of Dark Horse Entertainment's activity, Richardson sees numerous other applications for Dark Horse product. Dark Horse is developing a CD-ROM game simultaneously with the production of the films. Last year, Dark Horse oversaw production of the *TimeCop* CD-ROM and cartridge games that were distributed by JVC to coincide with the *TimeCop* video release. Other ideas in the works include television, stage shows, apparel, merchandising, and more games.